Heinemann
New Windmills

NO MORE SCHOOL?

Can you imagine life with no more school? A whole chunk of your life would be missing – no school bullies to get their come-uppance, no school dinners, no school outings, no more school friends to meet …

Each story in this collection is introduced by its well-known author, with memories of their school days.

VALERIE BIERMAN

NO MORE SCHOOL?

Heinemann
New Windmills

For all my friends at
Lasswade High School Centre

Heinemann Educational Publishers Ltd
Halley Court, Jordan Hill, Oxford OX2 8EJ
a division of Reed Educational & Professional Publishing Ltd

OXFORD MELBOURNE AUCKLAND
FLORENCE PRAGUE MADRID ATHENS
SINGAPORE TOKYO SÃO PAULO
CHICAGO PORTSMOUTH (NH) USA MEXICO CITY
IBADAN GABORONE JOHANNESBURG
KAMPALA NAIROBI KUALA LUMPUR

ISBN 0 435 12442 0

First published in 1991 by Methuen Children's Books Ltd
This volume copyright © 1991 Methuen Children's Books
First published in the New Windmill Series 1996

96 97 98 99 2000 10 9 8 7 6 5 4 3 2 1

Cover design by The Point

Typeset by Books Unlimited (Nottm) NG19 7QZ
Printed in England by Clays Ltd, St Ives plc

Contents

Introduction

Being asked to edit an anthology of stories is rather like being let loose in a favourite bookshop with a blank cheque! Imagine being able to ask your favourite writers to contribute a story, gathering the results together and shaping them into a book – especially when the theme is something everyone has lived through – school!

There have probably always been bullies around and Vivien Alcock's story has an eerie solution to a worrying problem. Douglas Hill's story also has a worrying problem in the shape of a school being eaten away by a mysterious bug from space and eating certainly looms large in Robert Swindells' truly stomach-churning tale about some very peculiar school dinners. Be warned – don't read this if you're about to have your lunch!

My own school experiences were similar to the children in Terrance Dicks' story *The Barrier* in that I remember with dread the horror of sitting the 'Scholarship' or the eleven-plus. A fate worse than death awaited if you failed – or so we were warned.

There are more unusual locations like the school in Alexander McCall Smith's story set in Africa where he himself was educated and Michael

Morpurgo has based his on the farm he runs in the West Country to give city children a taste of being a farmer. A white cat shows that life is not always what it seems, is it nor always pleasant, in Robert Westall's contribution, which demonstrates that we shouldn't take things at face value, unfortunately there's a darker side to life. Gene Kemp's story is sad with a happy ending – it's based on an incident which really happened to her when she was a teacher and met a girl like Smudge.

This collection is a bit like a school bag – you never know what you'll find hidden – dip into it and there'll be some surprises pleasant and some more unusual.

Valerie Bierman
Edinburgh 1991

Douglas Hill

The title of my story shouldn't be taken to mean that I'm against education. I like *school. Even as a child – in western Canada, where I was born and raised – I didn't mind school at all. (For one thing, it was a place to be with lots of other kids and also to be* warm, *in a Canadian winter. And we got nearly three months' summer holiday.) And nowadays, I enjoy school even more – because I get to travel around the country visiting schools, here and there, to talk to children about my writing.*

The school in the story is a bit like a school across the street from where I live, in London – which has an iron fence like a zoo cage around its playground. It's also a bit like a school in Hampshire that I visited while writing the story, where a kind teacher took me along to look at the boiler room. But mostly, Kevin's school is a fiction, existing only in my over-active imagination.

Just like everything else in the story – I'm very *glad to say.*

Two of Douglas Hill's most popular series of books are The Last Legionary *quartet and the* Colsec *trilogy.*

No More School?

In the spring, between Easter and half term, Kevin Barnes began to wish more than anything that he didn't have to go to school.

Kevin was a first-year in his local comprehensive, and for most of that year he hadn't minded school at all. But that spring everything changed. For Kevin, school became a place to keep away from. Not because he was bored or anything, but because he was *frightened* – by something only he knew about.

It had started one day before Easter, when Kevin was staring out of the classroom window. He was looking at a big tree just beyond the fence round the schoolyard. It was a half-dead sycamore that had been blasted during the winter by a windstorm *and* a bolt of lightning, at the same time. Or so people said. It was leaning halfway over, with some of its roots torn up, and Kevin had heard that it was soon to be chopped down because it was dangerous.

That would be something to watch from the window, he thought idly. And then, as he gazed at the tree, the sunlight hit something, at just the right angle, under the torn-up roots of the tree. It was something bright, catching Kevin's gaze, glinting like shiny glass or metal.

When it was time for break, he went out to investigate. The fence around the school playground was made of straight-up-and-down iron bars with sharp points on top, like the bars of a cage for animals. The bars were far enough apart to let some of the smaller first-years squeeze between them. They weren't supposed to do it, but they often did.

So Kevin squeezed through and went over to the tree.

'Where you going, Kev?' called one of his friends.

'You bunking off?' called another.

Paying no attention to them, Kevin stooped down and peered at the loose earth under the tree's torn-up roots. And there it was, the shiny thing that he had seen. Picking it up, he was pleased to see that it was much more interesting than broken glass or the lid of a tin. It was a metal object, very shiny and perfectly smooth, about the shape and size of a small egg.

Kevin had no idea what it could be. Then a weird idea came to him – that it was a mini-spaceship from another world, which had arrived with the lightning bolt that had blasted the tree. He smiled to himself, imagining the metal egg to be full of tiny green aliens, each about the size of a pinhead. As he smiled, he was turning the thing over in his hands, feeling its smooth shininess, rubbing and squeezing and twisting it.

And as he twisted it, it came open.

It fell apart in two bits, one bigger than the other. And there was something inside the bigger bit. Kevin shook it out into his hand and saw that it looked like a strange sort of *insect* – brown and shiny, curled up like a woodlouse and about the same size.

At that moment, it came alive. Its body uncurled, showing that its front half was thin and flat, with a tiny narrow head, while its back half was a bit larger and bulgier. On its head, a pair of feelers lifted up and began to wave around. And it seemed to have a great many short legs, as thin as hairs.

Suddenly the legs carried it in a fast scuttling run up over Kevin's wrist and on to his sleeve. Kevin was so startled that he nearly dropped the two parts of the metal egg. But at least the weird bug didn't seem to be the biting or stinging sort. And Kevin smiled again when the bug stopped its scuttling run and sat still on his sleeve, waving its feelers.

'Kev! Teacher's coming!'

It was his friend's voice, warning him. Looking up, he saw a teacher – on playground duty – walking slowly towards the fence. She hadn't seen Kevin, so he quickly scooped the bug back into the metal egg and tried to fit the two parts back together, while hurrying to the fence. He was startled again when the two parts went together easily and stayed together. And not the slightest mark showed on the smooth metal, where they had been joined.

Then Kevin slid the thing into his pocket and squeezed through the fence, still not spotted by the teacher. Waiting for him was the friend who had called the warning.

'What'd you pick up out there, Kev?' the other boy asked.

For a moment Kevin said nothing. Part of him wanted to share his discovery – but another part wanted to keep it secret. He knew what might happen if others found out about his strange bug inside its almost magical metal case. Adults, he thought, would probably waste no time taking it away from him.

So he shrugged. 'Nothing,' he said to the other boy.

'Come on! I *saw* you! You picked up something shiny!'

Kevin thought quickly. 'Oh, that,' he said, trying to sound offhand. Fishing in his pocket, past the egg-shaped bit of mysterious metal, he brought out a leftover bit of his pocket money. 'Found a ten p,' he said, holding it up.

'Lucky,' the other boy said, not sounding very interested, and wandered off.

For the rest of that day, Kevin was lost in his imagination, dreaming daydreams about his discovery. He was growing more sure that the bug was very special. And he daydreamed about how the bug might turn out to be a tiny and friendly alien being of great intelligence and magical powers, who would be Kevin's secret friend and helper …

He was still full of such imaginings when he got home after school and hurried into his room for another private look at his discovery. But when the metal egg came open, easily, and the bug scuttled out, he was almost disappointed. It clearly did *not* behave like a woodlouse-sized version of E.T.

It behaved just like any ordinary bug – scuttling around on its hairlike legs, waving its feelers, not doing much of anything.

But Kevin enjoyed playing with it. There seemed to be no danger that the bug would escape, for though it scuttled quite fast, it usually did so in short dashes. After each dash it would stop and wave its feelers, so that Kevin could easily gather it up.

Then he noticed that his bug left a faint trail behind it, like a snail's slime trail but thinner and lighter. Kevin began to worry that his mother would see the trails and make a fuss. He also grew worried when the bug got over to the wall and climbed up – because for once it didn't stop after a short dash but went on climbing. Kevin had to get up on his table and then on to his chest of drawers before he could reach up and grab it.

And when he picked it off the wall, he saw a line of marks on the plaster, like tiny holes. As if the bug's slime trail had somehow eaten away small bits of the plaster, along the way.

So he put it back into its metal egg and decided it would be better to play with it outside, where it wouldn't get him into any trouble.

The next day after school it rained. So Kevin left the bug in its case and spent some time trying to find out what *kind* of bug it was. But he had no luck. There were some picture books in his house about wildlife, even one that was all about insects – but nothing in any of the books looked at all like Kevin's bug.

Then he had another idea. That weekend he borrowed his father's Polaroid camera, which he had been shown how to use, and took a photograph of the bug – as close up as the camera could manage. Then on the Monday he took the photo to school, and showed it to Mr Cooper, a science teacher.

Mr Cooper seemed quite willing to help Kevin find out what some strange insect was called. But when he saw the photo, he just laughed.

'Oh, very good, Kevin,' he said. 'Part of it like a slug, part like a cockroach, legs like a millipede … What should we call it? A slug-roach-ipede?'

Kevin blinked. He was used to teachers saying weird things that they thought were funny, but he didn't understand why Mr Cooper was trying to be funny about the bug.

'If you made it yourself, you did a good job,' Mr Cooper went on. 'But it's just a bit too impossible. Or is it supposed to be a model of some alien monster?'

'No, it's …' Kevin began. But then he stopped, deciding that it might be best not to tell Mr Cooper about the bug. Not if it was *that* strange. So he just smiled vaguely, took his photo back, and wandered away feeling puzzled and amazed.

He was still feeling that way some days later, after spending a lot of time in the school library and the public library, looking at more books. In that time he had seen hundreds of pictures of weird and gruesome insects, but not one of them looked anything like his bug – his slug-roach-ipede, as Mr Cooper had called it.

'I think you really *are* from space,' Kevin told his bug the next afternoon. 'So I suppose I'll never know what kind of bug you are.'

He was sitting quietly among some low bushes

at the side of his house, keeping out of sight of his mother who was gardening and his father who was washing the car. The slug-roach-ipede was happily scuttling around on the bare earth, in its short breathless dashes.

'Maybe I should take you and show you to people at a TV station or something,' Kevin told it. 'I could get rich and famous. The Boy who Found the Bug from Another World.'

Then he got up quickly. The bug had started up the side of the house, and Kevin didn't want it to climb out of his reach. But it stopped after a short climb and sat still on the sun-warmed brick of the wall. Kevin saw that its head was moving in a strange way, just before he picked it off the wall.

Then he stared. Where the bug had been, a small round hole had appeared at the edge of one brick.

Frowning, Kevin put the bug back on to the wall. It scuttled a little way to the side, on to a very smooth brick. There it stopped, again with its head moving busily.

When Kevin lifted it away, he saw another, slightly larger hole in the smooth brick.

Kevin slid the bug back into the metal egg and sat thinking. He knew from the books that insects ate many different things. They ate leaves and fruit and flowers and each other. Some ate rotten meat, some ate wood, and he had even read of some that would eat rubber.

But he never had heard of a bug that ate bricks.

Or plaster – since he now had a good idea how his bug had made those small marks on the wall of his room.

It must be the only bug like it in the whole world,

Kevin thought. I *will* be rich and famous. And he began to dream an enjoyable daydream of appearing with his bug as the star guests on *Blue Peter*.

That was when his father found him and dragged him away to help with the car-washing. But he went on daydreaming all the rest of the weekend. And on the way to school on Monday he decided to tell some of his closest friends. Not that he wanted to boast or show off – not *really*. He just felt that his friends would be pleased to know how rich and famous he was going to be.

But at morning break, he thought that he should have one more trial run – just to be sure the bug would perform, before anyone else saw it. So he slipped around the corner of the school, away from the main playground. Unseen for a moment, he took out the metal egg and released the bug on to the brick wall of the school.

It behaved just as he hoped. It scuttled upwards a little way, then stopped, its tiny head moving as it began to eat. Grinning to himself, Kevin reached for it.

But perhaps the bug had had its meals interrupted by Kevin once too often. In any case, it scuttled away. And upwards, in an extra-long and high-speed dash.

A dash that took it high up the wall, out of Kevin's reach.

There it stopped, while Kevin vainly tried to jump up and grab it. And while he hissed and chirped and whistled and did everything he could – without making too much noise and attracting attention – to try to get it to come down.

But it didn't. It climbed higher – towards something like a small run-off pipe, jutting out of the brick wall.

'No!' Kevin shouted, no longer caring if anyone heard. But the cry had no effect. The run-off pipe didn't fit all that tightly, and the bug managed to squeeze itself into the tiny space between the pipe and the bricks.

And it vanished. Into the wall of the school.

Kevin felt sick and miserable all the rest of that day. After school, he went back to the same place to look around, hoping that the bug had come out again. But there was no sign of it. Kevin knew that the wall with the run-off pipe was one wall of the school boiler room, which was always locked. But even so he went and stared through the window of the boiler-room door. For a moment he thought he spotted the gleam of a slime trail, in one dim corner. But then the caretaker came along, and Kevin fled.

For several days after that, Kevin went back to the boiler room and peered in through that window. He also wandered around other parts of the school as well, looking for the slime trail of his lost bug, but the boiler room was his best hope. And it was there, finally, near the big boiler that heated the school, where he saw the sight that made him want to stay away from school.

It wasn't a slime trail. It was a *lot* of slime trails. Dozens of them, maybe hundreds, crisscrossing all over the floor and the brick walls of the boiler room. Along with dozens or hundreds of small smooth holes, all over the walls.

Somehow, Kevin knew, the freedom and the warmth of the boiler room had caused his bug to give birth to a lot of littler bugs. Dozens, maybe hundreds, of baby slug-roach-ipedes. Who might soon themselves grow up and give birth to many more babies. *Hungry* ones.

If there was any doubt about it, the doubt vanished one Monday morning soon afterwards. Everyone at school was talking about the weird vandals who had got into the school over the weekend and – for some reason – chopped away a large part of one brick wall in the gym.

It was a mystery why they had done that and nothing else, everyone said. It was also a mystery where the chopped-away bricks and mortar and brickdust had gone. And what the funny lines were, hundreds of them, all over the gym floor.

Kevin said nothing. He felt fairly sure that no one would believe him, then. And if people did come to believe him, later, they would *blame* him. Because he knew that something terrible was going to happen, and it was his fault.

He had let loose the bug that produced all the other bugs. Hundreds of them – maybe thousands or millions, before long – that all liked eating bricks. And that were loose in a building *made* of bricks.

Kevin was fairly sure that people would go on noticing the damage happening to the school walls. Teachers would keep the children out of school, when it started looking like the building might fall down. But Kevin was also sure – wretchedly, fearfully sure – that there was no way to stop that from happening.

He didn't even let himself *think* about what would happen if the bugs spread into the town, and the rest of the country, with all those brick build-ings. It was bad enough to think about what was happening right there in his own school building.

No one would ever be able to catch or kill those small, scuttling, brick-eating bugs. Not even if they found out about them. The bugs would hide by day in the walls of the school building, and when it was empty after school they would come out, and eat and eat. Until one day there'd be ...

No more school.

Michael Morpurgo

I suppose you could say I farm children. Every year about a thousand children from our big cities come to live and work on our farm in North Devon. This work has brought me into contact with thousands of children over the past fifteen years, and to a large extent they have been the inspiration for my books. Living as I do in a small isolated community I am able to feel how the villagers of Lescun felt in Waiting for Anya *and talking to the old men in the pub gave me the idea of* Warhorse.

The children come for a week, about forty at a time with their teachers, to discover what it is like to be farmers. They are out on the farm for most of the day – helping to milk the cows and clean down the parlour, feeding the pigs and calves, moving the sheep and bullocks, grooming the horses, feeding the poultry and picking up the eggs. In summer they help with the harvesting of the hay and straw; in the autumn they pick the apples and the potatoes; in winter they help with the lambing. In short, they do everything they can do within the bounds of safety. They have acres to play in, mountains of food to keep them going and hard bunk beds to sleep on – they're too tired to care whether they're hard or soft.

So what's all this for? Some time ago it became apparent to me that many children never experienced the countryside at first hand. They didn't know or care where their food came from or why trees are important. They learnt about cows and sheep, rivers and birds, wind and rain, but mostly from their television sets. I thought it was essential we should all feel part of the earth we so much depend on, that we should experience it in all its aspects, and so feel more in tune with it. That way lives are enriched and that way we should all want to care for the world around us because there could be one small part of it we loved and cared for. The idea of Little Foxes *came to me when I saw a child become so attached to one of our horses here that he was able to lose his stutter when talking to her.*

When I am not mucking out barns or milking cows with them I go home to my little room and write. Like all authors the greater part of the work is done through constant observation and recording; and just every now and then some small thing – a golden chrysalis perhaps, a glimpse of a heron rising from the river, or an overheard phrase triggers off an idea. Like an egg, if an idea is sat upon long enough then it will hatch out sooner or later into a story – but you mustn't let it go cold! I may do at least four drafts before trying it out on these poor guinea-pig children who come to the farm. One evening each week I go to read to them. I don't mind if they go to sleep – just so long as they don't snore.

Once a week the children go off to market to see the animals bought and sold. That's what Sam did. Read on.

Sam's Duck

Sam was a person of very few words, so when he said it was all 'brilliant' we knew he meant it. And that was strange because, of all of us, Sam was the one who least wanted to go.

It was just before Whitsun last summer and our class was herded into a coach one drizzly Monday morning. Along with Miss Dewar and a couple of other teachers we were off to spend a week on a farm in Devon. The school went there every year, and this year it was our turn.

Sam had his grandad there to see him off, a tall white-haired man who always carried a silver-topped stick in one hand – from his army days, Sam said. Everyone knew Sam's grandad; he collected him from school every day. But I knew both of them better than anyone because they live in the flat next door to us on the same corridor. For Sam, his grandad was not just his grandfather but his mother and father as well. Sam never said anything about it and no one dared ask; we just accepted that Sam lived alone with his grandad.

Sam's grandad was just about all that mattered to him; you could hear the pride in Sam's voice whenever he talked about him. Sam wasn't really crying as he rubbed the steam off the coach window and waved goodbye to his grandad. No one's ever seen Sam crying but he was as near to it then as I'd ever seen him, and he kept his face turned well away until we'd left London behind us.

Of course it was the first time away from home for most of us. I'd been to stay with my Aunt Brenda in Epping for a weekend, but just like everyone else, the only farms I'd ever seen were in picture books or on butter advertisements on the television. We soon discovered that things are not always as they show them on television.

It was mucky and smelly with mud up over the tops of our wellies, and hay down the back of our necks. But it was lovely. As Sam said, it was 'brilliant'. After the first night we never had time to think about home, or how far we were from London.

We never stopped. It was milking first thing in the morning before breakfast, and then cleaning down the dairy till it smelled all fresh again, and that took some doing. Then there was the long climb up on to the hills to feed the lambs, or mixing up the pig food – like cold porridge – and slopping it into the troughs. We fed the calves from the bottle and afterwards let them suck our hands till they were sore. We mucked out the chicken house and collected the eggs still warm from the hen. We had a hand in everything from grooming the horses to rounding up the sheep for market.

Our playground was acres and acres of fields and woods, we ate like kings and no one made us have a bath all week. Every day, Sam said, was more 'brilliant' than the one before. He never mentioned his grandfather – never, that is, until the last day, the day we were going off to the market.

Miss Dewar rang the bell like she did every morning after breakfast.

'Market day,' she said. 'We've got our farm work to do, then we'll be walking to the market in Hatherleigh. Not far.'

'How far, miss?' Jane Evers hated walking. She'd been moaning all week about her corns and verrucas and her flat feet.

'About three miles, maybe four,' Miss Dewar said patiently. 'You'll manage it, Jane.'

Jane went on moaning. 'Four miles there and back, miss, or is it four miles there and another four miles back?'

'It's about eight miles there and back,' said Miss Dewar as sweetly as she could.

'But, miss, my mum said I musn't walk any more'n I have to. I got verrucas, miss.'

'That's all right then, Jane. You'll be walking like the rest of us, just as far as you have to, not one step farther, and we're all walking into Hatherleigh for the market. If you don't feel like coming back, then maybe we'll sell you along with the sheep and the pigs. Right?' Miss Dewar had lost her patience.

Jane said no more and by noon that day we were all crowded round the auction ring watching the cows being sold off, one by one. In the middle of the ring was a red-faced man with a knobbly stick who kept prodding and jabbing at the cow whenever she stood still.

Sam kept muttering something about giving 'that red-faced loon' a prodding of his own, given half a chance. 'You can hear him hitting the bone,' he hissed.

And you could. She was a dreamy black and white cow with frightened eyes and, if the prodding wasn't effective enough, then the man would thwack her high up on the hip-bone to make her circle the ring. And the more successful he was, the harder he seemed to hit her, so that the poor animal was kept lurching violently round the ring, stopping every few seconds to search for a way out and never finding it. But the worst thing about it was that the little red-faced man was smiling, laughing out loud and showing off like a clown.

The microphone spluttered, whistled and came to life.

'Number fifty-four, gentlemen. A fine Friesian cow, guaranteed in calf to Mr Weldon's Devon bull. A third calver – am I right? – no. Take that back. She's a fourth calver. Averages six gallons. Fine, genuine animal. No vices. No bother to milk. Guaranteed quiet in the dairy. You can see for yourselves, gentlemen, there's a fine udder on her. Good strong animal then. What am I bid? Can't start at anything under two hundred pounds.'

'I'll kill him if he goes on hitting her,' Sam muttered fiercely. 'What's he doing it for? Why can't he leave her alone?'

'Two hundred I'm bid. And ten, two hundred and ten. Twenty, two-twenty. Cheap at this price, must be the cheapest cow in the county. Thirty, two-thirty. Thirty-five, two hundred and thirty-five pounds. Two-forty. Just between you two gentlemen now, at two-forty.'

The auctioneer was leaning into his microphone,

peering over the top of his glasses. I followed the bidding like a tennis match. Sam had eyes only for the little red-faced man.

'Two-fifty, two-sixty, two-seventy, two hundred and eighty pounds I'm bid. Two-eighty, three hundred pounds on my left. Mr Walker on my left at three hundred pounds. A fine animal for that money. At three hundred then … make it three hundred and five, sir, what's five pounds to a man like yourself? No? 'Tis a fine animal you're losing. To Mr Walker then at three hundred pounds. For the last time.' And he banged his pipe on the desk in front of him. 'Three hundred pounds to Mr Walker of Priory Farm. Next.'

The iron gates banged open but the wretched cow was facing the wrong way. Once again the little red-faced man laid into the cow until she pivoted round on her back legs, saw the opening, put her head down and made her escape, the man flourishing his stick after her in triumph.

We stayed watching the cows being auctioned for another ten or so cows. I was trying to spot the farmers bidding. I only spotted one of them who scratched his nose in a meaningful way and winked up at the auctioneer at the same time. As for Sam, he never took his eyes off the little red-faced man, and the more he showed off the more silent Sam became.

We ate our picnic amongst the tractors outside, and then Miss Dewar gave us half an hour free time to explore by ourselves. Sam pulled at my sleeve and we went off together away from the others.

'If my grandad was here,' he said, 'he'd kill that

man. He says that being cruel to animals is worse than being cruel to people. He says people can fight back but animals can't. He told me once that if he ever catches me pulling wings off daddy-long-legs and things like that, he'd tan me black and blue with his stick. And he would too.'

He was really upset, even an ice-cream cornet didn't quieten him down. He was as angry as I'd ever seen him. I led him off towards the stalls, hoping he wouldn't meet the red-faced man. No one ever seems to answer my prayers.

We were looking at the ducks and chickens. They were all shut up in little square cages with chicken-wire doors, and on each door there was a small notice – SOLD – in bright red letters. We were licking our ice creams and staring up at a large brown duck with bright eyes and kingfisher-blue wings huddled in the darkest corner of his cage. He stared back at us, immobile and unblinking.

'Look at his heart, Sam,' I said. 'You can see it pounding.' And I pushed my finger through the wire to see if he was friendly. He was just looking interested when we heard a rasping voice behind us.

'That's my duck you're interfering with, bought him this morning.' We turned. It was the little red-faced man, only now he wasn't so little close to. He had a hat on, a skimpy little trilby with a bright green feather sticking up the side.

Sam glared at him and I felt sure he was going to hit him. I stepped between them.

'What're you going to do with him?' I asked quickly, just for something to say.

28

'With my duck, y'mean? Well, what I normally do with a duck – I put him in the bath with me for a paddle.' He laughed till I thought he'd burst, and great blue veins stood out on his nose. A small crowd was gathering around us. 'Did you hear that? Did you hear? This lad, he asks me what I'll be doing with my duck!' He pushed me aside and opened the cage. 'I'll tell you what I'll be doing with him.' He reached in and grabbed the duck by the wings and hauled him out, dangling him in front of our faces. 'Supper! That's what you're looking at. My supper!' He changed his grip so that he held the animal by the feet, his head hanging down, and quacking plaintively. 'My supper to-morrow night. Now get out of my way.'

Sam stood his ground.

'What did you pay for him?' He faced him with clenched fists, white in the face.

'Pay for him?' The man seemed taken aback.

'How much?' Sam's voice was granite hard.

'Don't see as it's any of your business,' he said.

'Why not, Jack? 'Tis a fair question.' It was a voice from the crowd, and there were murmurs supporting it.

The red-faced man looked around him nervously. He was sweating.

'All right then. All right. I paid a pound and five p. That's what I paid.'

'Don't you believe him, son.' It was the same voice from the crowd. 'We was there, Jack. Give the boy a straight answer. 'Tis only what's fair. Come on now, Jack. Come clean if you can.' The crowd laughed in sympathy.

'I'll double whatever you paid,' Sam said quietly.

The duck swung helplessly by the feet, flapping feebly.

'Must be mad,' the man spluttered. ''Tis just a crabby old drake, no use to anyone.'

'Go on, tell him, Jack. Tell him.' The crowd seemed to move in.

'All right, all right. Sixty p, it was, and not a penny less. And you'll gimme double that, for this?' He held up the duck as if he was a dirty rag.

Sam turned to me. 'I got a pound. You got twenty p? I'll pay you back.'

I fished anxiously in my pocket and came up with a handful of loose change, a ball of sheep's wool and two disintegrated owl pellets.

Sam took the twenty p, put it together with his pound and handed it over. The man shovelled it all into a back pocket, and Sam took the duck from him without saying a word. I helped turn the duck the right way up and Sam cradled him firmly against his chest, stroking the smooth feathers between the darting eyes. When we looked up again, the little red-faced man was barging his way back through the crowd that was already turning away and breaking up.

'What're you going to do with him, Sam?'

He thought for a moment and then looked up and smiled at me.

'Present for Grandad,' Sam said. 'It's his birthday tomorrow, the day we get back home. He'll be seventy, and that's old.'

'But what about Miss Dewar? What's she going to say?'

'Nothing. Not if she doesn't know – and she won't. It's a secret, just between us. Right?'

'Right,' I said.

It's not easy to keep a duck a secret. Francis – (we called him Francis because he was a drake, and Francis Drake the explorer was born in Devon) – Francis fitted snugly into my Spurs duffle bag. Sam carried it all the way back to the farm, and we walked on ahead of the others just in case Francis needed to quack. From time to time a yellow-brown beak would pop out of the top of the duffle bag, but I was walking along just behind Sam's shoulder ready for this, and I pushed it down again as fast as it came up.

'Keep your pecker down, Francis,' Sam whispered.

And he did. There was never a quack and, when we finally got him back to the house, we ran round the back out of sight and emptied him into the gardener's tool shed by the vegetable garden.

'He'll be all right there for the night,' said Sam. 'We'll bring him some supper later.' He closed the door carefully, and we went back to the others before we were missed.

It was the last night and there was a sing-song around a crackling great bonfire that showered millions of orange sparks up into the trees above. We sang every song we knew, and some we didn't know, everything from 'When I first came to this land' to 'I got a brand-new combine harvester', and then all over again. The teachers drank cider and we had steaming hot chocolate.

We didn't want to leave the fire, but for Sam and me Francis was more important. So we sneaked away under cover of darkness to bring him his supper – brown bread saved over from tea time and soaked in Sam's hot chocolate. I groped for the light switch and flicked it down. Francis blinked up at us from his corner. He looked at us intently as Sam set the saucer down in front of him. Then he rose majestically, as if under hydraulic suspension, and waddled slowly towards it. He scooped it all up, down to the very last soggy crumb. Sam filled the saucer with water and Francis wasted no time, dipped, threw up his head and stretched his neck until he emptied his beak. And then again and again. At last, with a shake of his beak, he returned to his resting place on some old sacks and stared back at us as if he was wondering what was so interesting about a duck eating his supper. I swear that if ducks had tongues he would have licked his lips.

Sam and I lay awake most of the night trying to work out how we were going to hide Francis on the coach back to London in the morning, but by the time we climbed aboard after breakfast we still had no idea how we would manage.

'Make for the back seat,' Sam had said. We knew the teachers always sat in a huddle in the front, so the back was best. But with Francis stuffed down my Spurs duffle bag, and with the bag wedged firmly between my knees in the corner of the back seat, we both knew it needed only one single solitary quack from Francis and the game would be up. It was a long way to London, and neither of us dared imagine how many quacks Francis could fit in if he wanted.

For two hours or more Sam, Francis and I sat silently at the back of the bus. Francis kept poking his head up to have a look around, but for two hours he never gave us any trouble. Then we happened to stop for a rest at a motorway service station. Sam reckoned it would be safe, so we got off with the others and made for the gents, leaving Francis behind by himself in the coach. It was the fastest visit I'd ever made to the gents and we raced back to the coach before anyone else – or so we thought. Sam clattered up into the coach and I followed. Jane Evers was bending over the back seat; you could see her bottom up in the air. She was talking to Francis.

Sam walked the length of the bus on tiptoe. He tapped her gently on her back. Jane looked as if she had seen a ghost.

'I came back for my purse,' she said, swallowing hard. 'It quacked. I heard it. I was looking, that's all.'

Sam nodded slowly – like Al Capone. 'If you say anything …'

But it was too late for threats; there were already more people on the coach and Miss Dewar's voice sounded out.

'Hurry up and sit down at the back. We've no time to waste. No one can sit down till you move, Jane. Jane Evers, what are you doing back there? You were sitting up the front with the other sickies. You can't change places, there are no bags down the back of the bus. Come on. What are you crying for, Jane? There's no need to cry, I just want you to come back up here and sit down in your own place.'

Jane pushed past me, sniffing and heaving back her tears. We were done for, there was no doubt about that.

'Please, miss. Please, miss.' She could barely get it out. 'Please, miss, Sam's got a duck in his duffle. I seen it, miss. It quacks, miss, and he said if I said anything he'd kill me, miss.' Miss Dewar looked at her in complete disbelief. 'Honest, miss. It's true, Sam's got a duck in his duffle.'

'A duck in his duffle!'

'Yes, miss.'

'Sam!' Miss Dewar sounded tired and still disbelieving. 'Sam, have you got a duck in your duffle?'

'No, miss. Course I haven't. Don't know what she's on about. What would I do with a duck in my duffle?'

'He has, miss. I seen it, miss.' Jane was pointing back down the coach at us.

'Be quiet, Jane. That's enough. Sam, show me your duffle bag, please.' I wanted to close my eyes so as not to see what was about to happen.

Sam reached down and picked up his duffle. My Spurs duffle with Francis in stayed on the floor. I prayed with gritted teeth that Francis wouldn't choose this moment to quack. He didn't. Sam held his duffle aloft and turned it upside down so that all his sweets and things fell out. He smiled angelically at Miss Dewar.

'There, Jane. That's that! Ducks in duffle bags! Whatever next?' Jane gaped goldfish-like and began to cry again. 'That's enough, Jane. You've caused quite enough trouble.' And Miss Dewar ushered her impatiently down the coach. I sank down on the seat next to Sam and tried to laugh it all off – but I'm very bad at pretending to laugh, my lips go all stiff.

Francis muttered only once after that and luckily that was when the coach radio was at its loudest and no one heard except Sam and me. And so Francis came safely to London in my Spurs duffle bag. When we piled out of the coach at the school gates Miss Dewar was too busy with parents to bother with us, and Jane Evers was whisked away home. The last we saw of her she was still pointing back at the coach and explaining everything to her mother, who seemed much more interested in navigating a pram across the road.

I went home with Sam and his grandfather. My mum and dad never get home till after the six o'clock news. Every other word I heard was 'brilliant'. Sam was rabbiting on about the farm to his granddad, but every now and then he'd turn round and give me a great big confidential wink. Francis weighed a ton in my duffle bag.

The lifts were out of order again and we were climbing the stairs to our corridor. Sam left his grandfather behind and we walked on up together.

'Shall we give it to him now?' Sam whispered.

'What are you two muttering about?' His grandfather had paused for breath.

'Nothing, Grandad. It's nothing.' Sam looked at me and I nodded. 'You'll see, Grandad, soon as you get inside.'

Sam sat his grandfather down in his chair by the lamp, took my Spurs duffle bag carefully off my shoulder and put it gently down on the carpet.

'It's my birthday present for you, Grandad,' he said, reaching inside gingerly. 'I still owe twenty p on it, but I'll pay that soon as I get to my piggy.' He grinned up at me happily. 'Here he is,' he said. 'Isn't he brilliant?'

'He's called Francis,' I said.

Sam's grandfather looked from Sam to Francis and from Francis back to Sam.

'But it's a duck, a real live duck!' Francis quacked loudly just to prove it, blinked, and waddled off towards the kitchen.

'Happy birthday, Grandad.'

Sam's grandad shook his head and smiled.

'Sam,' he said, 'I swear to you I've never in all my seventy years had a present like that. He's lovely. He's a grand, grand duck – and I wouldn't mind betting you've been to a fair bit of trouble to get him here.' He paused and looked up at both of us, more seriously now. 'But Sam, we can't keep Francis up here. It's not right.'

'Why not, Grandad? He'd have killed him if we'd left him there. That man was going to eat him for his supper.' And Sam told him the whole story.

'Sam,' said his grandad. 'You did right to bring him away, and I'm that proud of you; but it's every bit as wrong to keep him all cooped up here in this flat as it is for him to be someone's dinner.' He spoke gently to Sam. 'A duck needs water, a pond or a river, and he should have the right food and he likes other ducks around him. That's only natural, isn't it, as it should be? Isn't that right?' He looked at me directly and I nodded.

Sam was quiet. He knew his grandfather was right – there was no denying it. Neither of us had given a moment's thought as to whether it was right or wrong. Everything had been done because it just seemed right at the time.

'At least that man didn't get him,' said Sam

softly, as Francis settled down by the television table as if he was about to join in the conversation.

That evening we fed Francis some more brown bread and hot chocolate, and Sam filled up the bath so that Francis could have a good soak. You should have seen the colour of the water by the time Francis had finished. He was still in the bath by the time my mum and dad came in looking for me; and as we went, Sam's grandfather said he'd worked out what we were going to do about Francis and that he'd come for me early next morning, very early.

I never remember London so quiet as it was that morning as we trudged over Westminster Bridge in the mist. There was a deep, dull silence, broken only by our footsteps and the odd lorry in the distance. We passed under Big Ben, which was cut off halfway up by the mist, then across Parliament Square and on through into Whitehall. Sam was carrying Francis in my Spurs duffle and he was peeping over the top, his head turning like the periscope of a submarine. As we crossed Whitehall he quacked loudly and the echo seemed to go on for ever.

'Here we are,' said Sam's grandfather, 'St James's Park.'

There are ponds in St James's Park, big ponds with islands and trees all around. Sam's grandfather said there were ducks and geese and all sorts, but so far we hadn't seen a single one. The three of us stepped over the wire fence and knelt down by the water's edge. Francis did not have to be asked twice. He flapped his wings, wiggled his tail feathers and walked straight in, settling himself easily into the water. He turned two full circles, faced us for a moment, then with easy underwater power he cruised out into the grey pond leaving ever-widening ripples in his wake.

'Bye, Francis,' said Sam.

'Bye,' I said.

We sat on the bench watching him explore his new kingdom. Shadows came out to meet him from all sides of the pond. There was a curious quacking commotion out in the middle and Francis became shadowy like the others.

'There goes your birthday present, Grandad,' Sam said. 'What'll I give you now?'

Sam's grandfather put an arm around both of us.

'Francis is still my birthday present,' he said 'and I couldn't wish for a better one, not in seventy more years. There's not many a man who can come here every day of his life and watch his own duck swimming on the Queen's own pond, and that's a fact. There's not many of us that lucky, is there?'

Gene Kemp

Gene Kemp was born in Wigginton, a small Midland village outside Tamworth, whose famous pigs she celebrates in The Prime of Tamworth Pig, *her first book for children.*

After several books about this wonderful pig and his friends, she broke new ground with her school story, The Turbulent Term of Tyke Tiler, *which was awarded the Library Association's Carnegie Medal. Later she was awarded an honorary Master of Arts degree in recognition of her achievement as a writer of children's books.*

Gene Kemp now lives in Exeter. She is married with three children and has three granddaughters.

The Girl who stayed for Half a Week

Nobody much noticed her come. Except for me and Miss. Nobody much noticed her go. Except for Miss and me. And that wasn't because of *her* but because I always noticed Miss. I liked to watch her. She reminded me of something – someone – somewhere, I couldn't quite remember, like the dream that slithers away out of reach when you wake in the morning and no matter how you try to bring it back it vanishes for good, not that Miss was going to disappear, varromph, gone (I hope). Or like that feeling that pulls you round the next corner just to see what's beyond, or run to the top of the hill when you can hardly get your breath because there might, there just possibly might, be something fabulous, fantastic, amazing, strange, wonderful, waiting there, just out of sight, on the other side, that was just the feeling Miss gave me.

Some kids hate their teacher. I nearly hated Mrs Baker last year. She always put me down: look where you're putting your feet, Michael, must your work be so untidy, so messy, Michael, do you have to take up so much room, Michael? I couldn't help being me and sprouting in all directions. I couldn't help growing. I didn't tell myself to grow. I just did. But in the end I didn't hate her, there being other things to think about. In fact I gave her a box of chocolates at the end of the year, though I didn't choose my favourites and five other kids gave her the same kind.

But Miss is something else. If Miss reads something you've written and she thinks it's good she smiles at the pages before she says anything as if she understands the meaning behind the words you wrote on the page, sad or frightening or funny. She's got grey eyes and curly brown hair and a curly grin with a crooked tooth and she's not very big so I reach things down from the shelves for her, being the tallest in the class though Greg Grubber is wider. Maybe that's because my dad's gynormous and feeds me on super grub (he's a great cook) or because he made me go to aikido classes and I'm a blue belt now. 'It'll help to stop you putting your great big hoofs everywhere and smashing everything,' he said. That was after Mum died, and I don't know whether I was crashing and smashing everywhere because of my feet or because there was just a big black hole that I kept falling into no matter what I did. But that's not what this story's about ...

It's about a girl who came and went and changed my life without knowing and I don't suppose I'll ever see her again to thank her, or even say hello. She came into our classroom in the middle of a Monday afternoon. I'd just looked up from the project I was doing (on oil) and there she stood by Miss's desk, a kind of smudge of a girl like a crayon drawing that Grubber might walk past and rub into rubbish with his elbow if he felt in the mood for a spot of aggro.

This girl looked as if someone had made quite a good job of her in the first place and then some toe-rag such as Grubber had rubbed her over, leaving her little and tired and pale and a bit dirty with a light turned off somewhere. Everyone in the room seemed busy – the projects were to be handed in by Tuesday – so I was the only one watching as Miss talked to her, because I'd looked up to see if Miss was OK.

You're saying, you out of your tiny deformed mind, then? You might be big in the body but you've obviously got a brain the size of a pea. Look, idiot face, your teacher's supposed to *look after you*, not the other way round, OK. And yeah, we know you lost your mum, sorry, that was bad but does it have to mean you have to mooch round after your teachers like a camel with toothache?

I know all that, me, Michael Haines, I know all about it, so you can just leave the preaching and accept that I raised my eyes and saw this deprived-looking kid drooping by Miss's desk as if she'd rather be anywhere else at all in the whole world even if it meant being dead or something. Miss was smiling at her as she does and I know she'd be asking her name, and how old, and did she like reading and so on, I've heard her with other new kids. She was welcoming, smiling at her as if she was wonderful, all smudgy as she was, the kid, not Miss.

So I decided I'd wander up to that desk to borrow the stapler – not that I needed the stapler just then but it made a good excuse. We've only got one in the classroom and you have to ask for it ever since Grubber tried to staple one of the mice from the Environment Area to a piece of card. When I got to the desk I heard Miss say, 'You needn't read to me this afternoon if you're tired.' And this girl, who just about came up to my knees, making me wonder what she was doing in our class (one of four top-year ones) gazed into Miss's face, then put down her head so her tatty hair fell everywhere, climbed on to Miss's knee, stuck her thumb in her mouth and her head on Miss's shoulder.

Now I knew I'd got to conceal this awful sight from some of our class members, Grubber not being the only one with a Heavy Metal inside, so I positioned myself between them and the class. Then Miss put her gently down, but still holding her hand, stood up and told all of us to put our things away.

'We'll have a story and a poem for the end of the afternoon,' she said.

So we did. She read to us about a boy who went into a garden at midnight and what he found there. We sat and listened, even Grubber. He enjoys stories more than he admits.

'Anything's better than work, dog's breath,' he says.

The girl hadn't yet got a seat to sit down on. She stood by Miss, holding her baggy sweater as if she might fly straight off Planet Earth if she let go, or sink down beneath the school through the foundations and the rocks below right down to the fiery centre of the planet. Then after a few minutes she climbed back on to Miss's knee, stuck her thumb in her mouth and her head on Miss's shoulder and this time stayed there as if she'd arrived home and wasn't leaving it ever. Funnily enough, no one took any notice, as if they were just too lost in the story and she was part of it.

Next day she came late, and was given her desk and books and so on. Later Miss heard her read and checked her maths and writing etc. at her desk. And as we did our work she stayed there as if she never wanted to leave that place. At playtime I got ready to flatten Grubber if he started any of his funnies but there was no need. She stayed in. So did Miss, and anyone else who wished.

At the end of the afternoon, after clearing up, Miss brought out the story. The girl climbed on to her lap and held her as before.

On the fourth day Grubber at last registered she was there and went up to where she was doing her work at the side of Miss's desk. Miss was with a group in the far corner of the room.

'What's all this, then?' asked Grubber, in a voice like a Rottweiler with laryngitis. 'How come you gits doin' your rubbish 'ere. You ain't no special right 'ere. Git lost, vomit.'

Now, Grubber and me, we've always scrapped. Yes, all the way up from toddler group, play group, Infants and through to the Middle. We fought at two, three, four, five, six, seven, eight, then at nine I started to go to aikido. After that he couldn't win any more though that didn't stop him trying. No style, though, no discipline, only size and power. Yeah, Grubber's got that. Power.

And he intended using it. He meant to turf out

little Smudge from her safe place by Miss's chair. He fancied doing that. Not that he wanted to be there himself, oh no, the further he was from any teacher the better but if this new kid wanted to be there that wouldn't do. Grubber couldn't have that. She'd have to move. He got ready to move her.

But I was there first.

'She can work here if she wants to.'

'What's with you, snail slime?'

We were both shouting in whispers now ...

'Leave her alone.'

'Get lost, sewer.'

... in case Miss heard. If she hadn't been in the room there would've been a scrap but ...

The sound of feet running down the corridor outside.

A scream.

Another scream. 'Stop him!'

A bell. A buzzer. 'Ring for the police!'

More running feet.

More screams. Louder now. And louder.

The door burst open. Miss stood up and came out of her corner.

The woman who'd rushed in, white, scared, looked round, ran to little Smudge by the desk, grabbed her and raced *behind* Miss.

'Save me! Save me!' she was babbling.

A man burst in, as red as she was white, big, angry, bald, shirtsleeves flapping.

Miss held out her arms.

'Stop!' she cried.

He went to shove her aside.

'I'm going to get you. You're coming home with

me,' he shouted, and pushed Miss away. She crashed into a desk.

My stomach did a freefall.

So among the shouts, the screams, the bangs, I looked at Grubber and Grubber nodded back. Like friends for ever and always we moved in. Grubber chopped him in the back. I high-kicked him just where it hurts.

He went down and we sat on him. So did half the class as into the room poured the school secretary, the head teacher, several helpers and most of the other fourth years.

The head teacher hauled the man to his feet. He looked a bit shattered, as well he might. There seemed to be hundreds of people in our classroom as the police arrived. And then the woman threw her arms round him and he put his arms round her. They were both crying. In the confusion I think only two people noticed little Smudge slip out of the room. Me and Miss. Miss called out and I tried to follow but there were too many people and too much noise.

The next day was Friday. At the end of it Miss went on with *Tom's Midnight Garden*. We sat quiet and subdued. The girl hadn't appeared. At the end of the afternoon I went up to Miss where she sat looking as sad as she had that time Julie Trent had asked why she wasn't wearing her pretty ring any more. Things didn't work out, that's why, Julie, she'd said, things don't always work out.

'Why didn't that girl come?' I asked.

'Oh, she won't be coming here any more. She

46

was staying at the Refuge, but they've all gone back home now, a good thing, I expect. I hope.' She didn't sound at all sure.

'You liked her a lot, didn't you, Miss?'

'Yes, I did. Well, it's Friday, Michael, and time to go.'

My father stood at the door. He hadn't been into school so far this term because of his working hours. He strode towards Miss.

'I had to come to see you,' he said to her, 'to see what really happened yesterday. I heard a most extraordinary story from Michael. I haven't seen him so upset for ages.'

She told him, but it seemed to me that what they were really doing was looking at each other as if they'd just seen a miracle, and what they were saying wasn't all that important.

Somebody nudged me.

'You comin', then? Thought you might like to try out me new bike.'

It was Grubber. We ran out together.

Oh yeah, they got married, my dad and Miss, some time later, when I'd gone to my next school with my mate Grubber.

As a mum she's not the dream round the corner or the something fantastic on the other side of the hill, but she's OK. She'll do. Sometimes she gets a funny look though, and I get this odd feeling that she's remembering the girl who only stayed for a week and looked as if she'd been smudged.

Alexander McCall Smith

I remember exactly when I heard about the old miner called Charlie. I was thirteen and had gone, with a friend and his family, for a weekend trip out into the bush. My friend, who was at a boarding school, said that there was an old miner in the hills who was called Charlie and who haunted the school grounds. He told me the story of Charlie at night, which made us both rather frightened, as all this happened in the middle of Africa.

I was brought up in a town called Bulawayo, in Zimbabwe. I went to school there over twenty years ago. We lived about five miles from the school, right on the edge of the town, and our house was on the edge of the grass plains that circled the town. If you travelled a short distance south – only fifteen miles or so – you came to the hills of the Matopos, a great range of granite hills in which there were ravines and caves, with leopards and baboons. I think these are the most exciting hills in Africa.

In some of these hills, or on the veld *(plains) around them, there were small gold mines. You could come across these quite easily. Some of them were still worked – by no more than one or two men – others were long deserted. Looking at the deserted ones made me wonder about the lives that these old miners led. They were a tough breed, and many of them died when their tunnels collapsed. Charlie must have been one of these.*

I have been lucky. Although I now live in Edinburgh, every year I have been able to go back to southern Africa. More and more, in the books I write for children or in the stories I write for adults, Africa seems to want to come back to me. It is there, most clearly, in Children of Wax, *a collection of traditional Matabele stories. It is there in* Akimbo and the Elephants, *which is all about the tragedy of elephant-poaching. Here it is again.*

The Night We Looked for Charlie

'Have you ever heard about Charlie?' my friend Nick whispered to me one night.

It was dark in the dormitory, and everybody else was asleep. Nick's bed was next to mine so we could talk without being overheard. Sometimes at night, particularly in the hot season when it was difficult to get to sleep, we would talk late into the night, although it was against the rules. It was that sort of school, I suppose. There were all sorts of rules which did not seem to have much point but which nobody would ever dream of changing. Boarding schools used to be very much like that – particularly this rather old-fashioned boarding school on the edge of those great dry plains of Africa.

I said nothing for a moment. Outside the building there was the sound of the cicadas, a shrill sound of screeching insects that would continue until dawn. I asked Nick who Charlie was.

'Charlie's a miner,' he said. 'Or rather, Charlie *was* a miner a long time ago.'

'Tell me about him,' I asked. I was far from sleepy and Nick's question had aroused my curiosity.

I lay still as Nick told the story, his voice quiet in

the darkness. If you try listening to somebody talking in the dark you'll find that it's very easy to listen. There's nothing to distract you from what is being said. There's just the voice.

Nick explained that in the hills that lay to the north of the school there were numerous old mine workings. These were tunnels which had been dug in the days when gold had been mined there. Then the gold had run out and the miners had left, but they had done nothing about the shafts which went deep into the ground. One or two of them had rusted old fences about them, and some had collapsed or filled with water. Many of them were still there, though, and this was the reason why we were forbidden to go into the hills.

Charlie had been a miner years ago who had come across a very rich vein of gold. The vein of rock in which this gold was found rose briefly to the surface and then dipped deep into the heart of the hills. Charlie soon recovered a great deal of gold from the shallower part, but after his lucky strike he had to dig deeper and deeper.

'He did not have very much equipment,' Nick said. 'All that he used to go down into the depths of his shaft was an old bucket lowered by a winch. One of his men turned the handle and down he went in the bucket, at the end of a rope.'

'He must have been brave,' I whispered.

'They all were,' Nick said. 'My grandfather knew some of them. He told me that they never got scared, no matter how deep they went.'

Nick paused. 'Charlie was very brave,' he went on. 'But it didn't save him. There was a rock fall in the tunnel he dug and he never came up again.

They called some of the other miners to come and help rescue him, and they dug through the rock fall into the tunnel beyond. But they never found him.'

'But what happened?' I asked. 'Where had he gone?'

'Nobody knows,' said Nick. 'There were a whole lot of tunnels down there. Maybe he wandered into another tunnel and got lost. Maybe he fell down a shaft. But nobody ever saw him again.'

I was silent. For a few moments Nick said nothing more, then he finished his story.

'But he's still there,' he whispered. 'My brother knew somebody who saw him a few years ago. Or saw his ghost rather. It was him. It was definitely Charlie.'

I felt a cold chill touch at me. I didn't believe in ghosts – or did I? I suppose I wasn't sure.

'Where?' I asked. 'Where did whoever it was see him?'

'He went up beyond the top games field,' Nick whispered. 'He went up with one or two others for a dare one night. They were looking into one of the mine tunnels when suddenly they felt that there was someone there. They turned round. He was standing not far away, holding a shovel. Then he seemed to fade away, right before their eyes. They ran all the way back – non-stop.'

I found it difficult to get to sleep after Nick had told his story and throughout the next day the tale kept going through my mind. As I sat in the classroom, my gaze wandered out of the window. There were the gum trees, and there were the top games fields. And then, just beyond the fields the hills started, with their dry, boulder-strewn flanks. And their tunnels. And Charlie.

I decided to find out whether any of the others had heard of Charlie, and it turned out that they had. Everyone seemed to know somebody who knew somebody who had seen him. Stories about ghosts or strange happenings are always a bit like that. You never meet anybody who has seen something himself – it's always somebody else.

Slowly I learned a bit more about Charlie. It seemed that what Nick had said was true – he always carried a shovel – and that he had a miner's cough. Old miners coughed badly, because of all the dust, and you often heard Charlie before you saw him. Or so they said.

I wondered if Charlie was still around. Most of the stories about him seemed to be rather old, and I thought that he might have given up his appearances by now. Perhaps ghosts retired after a while, once they became bored with wandering about. It could not have been much fun walking about the school grounds, carrying a shovel and coughing. Then, one day, somebody saw Charlie, and this time I heard the story directly from Gordon, the boy who saw him.

Gordon was a year or so younger than I was. He had only been at the school for a couple of terms, but even in that short time he had made a reputation for himself. He was very good at sports, but he was also an open, honest person – not the sort to make something up – and that's why I chose to believe him when he told me what had happened.

It was a Saturday evening. I belonged to the chess club, which sometimes met on Saturday evenings in one of the classroom blocks. This was some distance away from the hostels, and was surrounded by a stand of giant gum trees which had been planted many years before when the school was first built. These trees made a strange sound when the wind blew through their branches. It was a hushing sound – rather like the sound made by waves in the sea.

There were four chess games being played that night, and I had drawn Gordon as opponent. Our game was taking a long time to finish, and I wondered whether it would end in stalemate. The others had packed up and gone back to the hostels, but the master in charge of the club had told us that we could finish our game. Then we were to turn off the lights and go back to our dormitory.

It was my move. I could not think what to do and sat there with my head in my hands, studying the board. Gordon sighed.

'This is taking ages,' he said. 'I'm going to stretch my legs.'

He got up from the table and walked over towards the open door. Outside there was nothing but the blackness of the African night. He stood in the doorway for a few moments and then I heard him gasp.

I looked up. He was still standing with his back to me, but I knew immediately that something was wrong.

'What's going on?' I said, rising to my feet.

He turned round. His expression was frozen, his skin drained of colour.

'I saw … ' His voice faltered. 'I saw … '

It seemed as if it was impossible for him to finish what he wanted to say.

'I saw … Charlie!'

I could not think of anything to say, but I dashed over to where he had been standing in the doorway and looked out into the night. There was no moon, and so I could see very little. But I did feel something I had never felt before – a terror so real and overwhelming that it made my heart thump like a hammer within me.

Without a word, we packed up our chess board and pieces and then turned out the light. Then came the hardest part, which was to close the door behind us and run back through the trees to our dormitory. We looked to neither side of us, nor behind us; our gaze was fixed on the distant, friendly lights of the dormitory and of safety.

Gordon did not say anything more that night, but the next day he came up to me after breakfast and told me more about what he had seen.

'It was definitely him,' he said. 'He was right there in front of me, looking at me, or, rather, looking *through* me. Then suddenly he wasn't there any more.'

I thought about Charlie a lot after that. Then, a few weeks later, when Nick and I were watching a cricket match one Saturday afternoon and nothing much was happening on the field, I told him what I had in mind.

'I want to see if Charlie really exists,' I said.

'Gordon's sure he saw him – and I believe him. So I think we should look for him.'

Nick turned and stared at me.

'What do you mean?' he asked.

I lowered my voice, although there was really nobody about to hear what we were saying. 'I think we should go out one night,' I explained. 'We could go out to the mine workings and see if he appears.'

Nick's eyes were wide. 'Ourselves?' he stuttered. 'At night?'

I nodded. I must have seemed very brave to him, but I didn't feel at all brave inside. But I had made the suggestion now and I felt that I had to stick to it.

'Well?' I challenged. 'You're not scared, are you?'

Nick swallowed hard. 'Not if you aren't,' he said quietly.

And with that, the plan was hatched and it only remained for us to decide when we were going to do it.

'I think we should go tonight,' I said after a few moments. 'There was a full moon last night and so we should be able to see quite well.'

Nick nodded. He was scared, and so was I, although neither of us was prepared to admit it – just yet.

Mr Anderson, our housemaster, was early that night and called out 'Lights' three minutes before he should have done. There was a mad scramble as everybody made their final preparations for bed and then there was darkness. I tucked myself into my bed, shivering with anticipation. Nick and I had planned to wait an hour before we set off, and had our clothes all ready under our beds.

The minutes dragged by. My watch had a luminous dial and I could see the position of the minute hand, slowly working its way round the dial. At twenty-past eight I decided that I could wait no longer. I whispered across to Nick, who answered me immediately.

'Time to go,' I said. 'If you still want to … '

'Of course I do,' he whispered back, as he slipped out of bed and began dressing in the dark.

We were both ready within a minute or so. Then, still in stockinged feet for silence, we crept out of the dormitory and into the long corridor outside. The doors were always kept unlocked – in case there was a fire – and soon we were out of the building and standing in the strange, half-darkness of the moonlit night.

Neither of us said anything as we began the walk up towards the top playing field. The school grounds looked so different at night. Everything was bigger, and more threatening. The gum trees seemed to tower impossibly high above us; the buildings were squat, black shapes, like stranded whales; everything which was so comfortable and familiar by day was sinister and unknown at night.

We skirted round the first of the classroom blocks. There was a light on in one of the rooms, and we didn't want to be seen. Nobody should have been around at that hour, as the teachers would long since have gone home to their bungalows. People left lights on, though, and I thought that that's what must have happened.

We crossed over the road that led to the bungalows. We were now not far from the very edge of the school grounds and we could already make out the dark tangle of the undergrowth that marked the limits of the top playing field. I was surprised at how much light there was – not enough to see very far, but certainly enough to make out individual bushes and holes in the ground.

We stopped at the edge of the field.

'Do you know where to go?' Nick asked. 'I've never been further than this.'

I shook my head. 'No,' I confessed. 'But as long as we go slowly it'll be all right.'

'What about the mine shafts?' Nick said, his voice quiet beside me. 'Lots of them are still open. We have to be careful not to fall in.'

I knew he was right. This was the reason why we were forbidden to go there. It would have been much more sensible to turn back then, and to give up the whole, ridiculous idea of seeing Charlie, but I was determined not to appear cowardly in front of Nick.

'Walk right behind me,' I said. 'I'll look out.'

We started into the bush. As we made our way, I felt my heart thumping with fear. Inside me, somewhere within, a voice was saying quietly, insistently: 'Turn back! Turn back!' I ignored it.

Suddenly Nick touched my arm. 'I heard something,' he whispered.

I strained to listen. There were the usual sounds of the African night, the faint screeching of insects somewhere, but nothing else. Nick had left his hand where it had touched my arm and I felt it trembling.

'Are you frightened?' I asked. 'I can feel your hand shaking.'

'Yes,' he whispered. 'I am.'

I swallowed hard. 'So am I,' I said. Then: 'I don't

think it's such a good idea to look for Charlie after all.'

Nothing more was said, we just turned around and began to make our way back slowly and carefully, conquering the terrible temptation to rush headlong home, away from the dark hills and the secrets which they were welcome to keep.

We were much less frightened by the time we reached the playing field and when Nick grabbed me by the arm again I thought that he was just fooling around.

'Look!' he hissed. 'Get down! Get down!'

I obeyed him instinctively, dropping to the ground alongside him. Then I looked around and saw what had disturbed him. There, coming directly towards us along the road that led to the bungalows, was a solitary figure.

'Charlie!' I whispered. 'It must be Charlie!'

Nick said nothing. We were both paralysed with fear and couldn't move.

The figure was now a bit closer. I strained my eyes trying to make out more details of the ghost. Where was the shovel? And why had we not heard the cough? Then the answer came.

'It's Mr Anderson,' Nick hissed. 'And he's going to see us.'

It is possible that the housemaster heard Nick, for he suddenly stopped and looked about him. We had dropped down at the edge of an irrigation ditch and this is probably what saved the day for us. He saw us all right, but I think that he only saw half of us, or perhaps even only half of one of us. And at the very moment that he gave a start and peered in our direction, fumbling to switch on his torch, Nick deliberately gave a cough.

It was the cough that did it. Mr Anderson's arm shot up in the air and the torch fell to the ground with a thud. Then, uttering the most extraordinary cry of alarm, the terrified housemaster ran as fast as he could up towards the bungalows and safety.

Nick and I stayed where we were for a few moments.

'He thought you were … ' I began.

'Charlie,' finished Nick.

And then we laughed, and our muffled laughter continued all the way back to the boarding house.

Mr Anderson always had breakfast with us, and Nick and I studied him closely the next morning as he sat at the head of one of the refectory tables. He seemed thoughtful, and Nick and I exchanged glances.

Later that day, Mr Anderson took us for a geography lesson and afterwards, as we were packing up our books, Nick went up to his desk and spoke to him.

'Do you believe in ghosts, sir?'

I watched Mr Anderson's expression very closely and knew that the question had surprised him. 'Ghosts?' he said, too jovially. 'Of course I don't!'

'Are you sure, sir?' Nick went on. 'It's just that people say there's an old miner round here. They call him Charlie.'

Mr Anderson rose to his feet. 'Come, come, Nick,' he said. 'Don't you worry about this Charlie. He's quite harmless, I'm sure.'

'So you do believe in him, after all!' crowed Nick. Then he added: 'You haven't seen him, have you, sir?'

Mr Anderson was silent. I thought he looked a little bit pale. 'Well ... ' he faltered.

And then Nick produced Mr Anderson's torch.

'I think this is yours, sir,' he said. 'You dropped it after you saw Charlie.'

The housemaster's jaw sagged. Then, very slowly, he took the torch and slipped it into his pocket. I knew then that he understood what had happened, and I waited anxiously to see what he would do. We could get into serious trouble for having been out at night, but then, if we were punished, people would know that Mr Anderson had run away from a ghost.

'Let's just forget all about it,' said Mr Anderson, smiling. 'You agree not to go out when you shouldn't, and I'll agree to be a bit braver if I ever see the real Charlie.'

'Agreed,' said Nick.

Robert Swindells

I was born in Bradford in 1939. I started school in 1944. The Second World War was on. Everybody had a peg on the classroom wall to hang their gas mask on. We did gas drill and shelter drill, but we were only five so we didn't know what it was all about. Then one day the headmistress came in crying. We'd never seen an adult cry before. She whispered something to our teacher, Miss Hopkinson, and she started crying too. 'Children,' she sobbed, 'the war is over, and you can all go home.' We walked up the street and there were women everywhere, laughing, crying, hugging one another. I was a bit scared. It was like all the grown-ups had gone barmy.

So, no more drills, no more gas masks. We still took our gas mask cases though, with a jam buttie inside which we called 'lunch' and ate at ten o'clock, washing it down with cod liver oil and orange juice.

When we were a bit older the orange juice stopped, and after that I only liked two things at school – English, and going home. I failed my eleven-plus exam and left at fifteen. Two things I remember from school are: some truants from an-other school throwing a dead cat in through an open window one hot summer's day when Miss Lewis was conducting a divinity lesson, and Mr Gledhill my English teacher, who liked my stories and said I might be a writer.

I didn't want to be a writer. I wanted to be a Spitfire pilot or a red deer stag. I tried a lot of jobs and ended up as a writer, so maybe Mr Gledhill was right. Maybe. Everybody needs a dream though, and you never know – I still might get to be a red deer stag some day.

Two of Robert Swindells' favourite books of his own are The Ghost Messengers *and* Room 13.

What's for Dinner?

'It's Friday,' Sammy Troy complained. 'Fish and chip day. Why are we having shepherd's pie?'

'I don't know, do I?' said Jane. They were twins but Sammy was ten minutes younger and ten years dafter. Jane spent half her time at school keeping him out of trouble. She swallowed a forkful of the pie. 'It's very tasty anyway. Try it.'

Sammy tried it. It was good, but he wasn't going to admit it. He'd been looking forward to fish and chips and shepherd's pie just wasn't the same. He pulled a face.

'Pigfood.'

'Don't be silly,' said Jane, but she knew he would be. He usually was.

Sammy left most of his dinner, and in the playground afterwards he made up a rap. It was about the school cook, and it went like this:

'Elsie Brook is a useless cook
If you eat school dinners it's your hard luck
They either kill or make you ill
If the meat don't do it then the custard will.'

It wasn't true. Mrs Brook did good dinners, but the rap caught on and a long snake of chanting children wound its way about the playground with Sammy at its head. Jane didn't join in. She thought it was stupid and hoped Mrs Brook wouldn't hear it.

On Saturday, Sammy practised the rap with some of his friends. They meant to get it going again at break on Monday, but at the end of morning assembly the head said, 'I'm sorry to have to tell you all that our Mrs Brook was taken ill over the weekend and will not be here to cook for us this week.'

Some of the boys grinned and nudged one another. Sammy whispered in Jane's ear, 'She must've eaten some of that shepherd's pie.' Jane jabbed him with her elbow.

'However,' continued the head, 'we are very lucky to have with us Mr Hannay, who will see to our meals till Mrs Brook returns. Mr Hannay is not only a first-class chef but an explorer as well. He has travelled as cook on a number of expeditions to remote regions, and is famous for his ability to produce appetizing meals from the most unpromising ingredients.'

'He'll feel at home here, then,' muttered Sammy. 'We have the most unpromising ingredients in Europe.'

A chef, though! A first-class chef. Morning lessons seemed to drag on forever. It felt like three o'clock when the buzzer went, though it was five to twelve as always. Hands were washed in two seconds flat, and everybody hurried along to the dining area which was filled with a delicious mouth-watering aroma. Snowy cloths covered all the tables, and on each table stood a little pot of flowers. 'Wow!' breathed Jeannette Frazer. 'It's like a posh restaurant.'

And the food. Oh, the food. First came a thick, fragrant soup which was green but tasted absolutely fantastic. To follow the soup there was a beautiful main course – succulent nuggets of tender white meat in a golden, spicy sauce with baby peas and crispy roast potatoes. And for pudding there were giant helpings of chocolate ice cream with crunchy bits in it.

Sammy licked the last smear of ice cream from his spoon, dropped the spoon in his dish, pushed the dish away and belched. Some of the boys giggled, but his sister glared at him across the table. Sammy smiled. 'Sorry, but what a meal, eh? What a stupendous pig-out. I'll probably nod off in biology this aft.'

He didn't though. Miss Corbishley didn't give him the chance. The class was doing pond life, and when they walked in the room the teacher said, 'Jane and Sammy Troy, take the net and specimen jar, go down to the pond and bring back some pond beetles and a water boatman or two. Quickly now.'

The school pond lay in a hollow beyond the playing field. Rushes grew thickly round its marshy rim and there were tadpoles, newts and dragonflies as well as sticklebacks and the beetles they'd study today. It was Sammy's favourite spot, but today all the creatures seemed to be hiding. No dragonflies darted away as the twins waded through the reeds. No sticklebacks scattered like silver pins when Jane trawled the net through the pondweed, and when she lifted it out it was empty.

'Try again,' said Sammy. 'Faster.'

Jane sent the net swooping through the underwater forest, but all she got was a plume of weed.

'Everything seems to have gone,' she said. 'And Miss is waiting.'

'I know,' said Sammy. 'She'll think we've wagged off school.'

'Don't be ridiculous!' cried Miss Corbishley, when Jane told her there was nothing in the pond. 'Only this morning Mr Hannay was saying what a well-stocked pond we have at Milton Middle.' The twins were sent to their seats in disgrace, while Jeannette Frazer and Mary Bain went to try their luck. Miss Corbishley made a giant drawing of a water boatman on the board and the children began copying it into their books.

'Hey, Jane!' hissed Sammy. His sister looked at him. He had a funny look on his face. 'I've just had a thought.'

'Congratulations,' she whispered. 'I knew you would some day.'

'No, listen. You know what Miss said, about Mr Hannay?'

'What about it?'

'He said the pond was well stocked, right? And now it isn't. And we had that fantastic dinner, only we didn't really know what it was?'

'What's dinner got to do with – ?' Jane broke off and gazed at her brother. She shook her head. 'No, Sammy. No. That's sick. It's impossible.'

'Is it?' Sammy jabbed a finger at her. 'What was that soup, then? Green soup. And the meat. And those crunchy bits in the ice cream – what were they?'

Before Jane could reply, Jeannette and Mary came back with long faces and an empty jar.

Walking home that afternoon Jane said, 'It's a co-incidence, that's all. It can't be true what you're thinking, Sammy.' She wasn't sure though, and Sammy certainly wasn't convinced. 'I wonder what we'll get tomorrow?' he said.

Tuesday's dinner turned out to be every bit as delicious as Monday's. The twins had kept their suspicions to themselves, so there were no spoilt appetites as the children settled down to eat. Even Jane and Sammy felt better. After all, even Mr Hannay couldn't conjure food from an empty pond.

The soup was orange and there were no lumps in it. It had plenty of flavour though, and everybody enjoyed it. The main course was Italian – mounds of steaming pasta and a rich, meaty tomato sauce. 'If this is how they eat in Italy,' said Sammy, 'I'm off to live there.' He seemed to have forgotten about yesterday. Jane hadn't, but she knew macaroni when she saw it, and this was definitely macaroni.

Tuesday afternoon was C.D.T. with Mr Parker. When the kids arrived he was kneeling in front of his big cupboard, surrounded by a mountain of dusty old drawings, and broken models made from balsa wood and cardboard boxes. 'Lost something, sir?' asked Sammy.

'Some pictures I did with a first-year class three, maybe four years ago. Collage pictures.'

'What are they, sir?'

'Oh, you know – you stick things on a sheet of paper to make a picture. Seashells, lentils, bits of macaroni. Any old rubbish you can find, really.'

Sammy gulped. 'Bits of macaroni, sir?'

'That's right.'

'Four years ago, sir?'

'Yes. I'm sure I saw them at the back of this cupboard quite recently and made a mental note to clear them out before the mice got to them.'

'Are there mice in your cupboard, sir?' There was a greenish tint to Sammy's face.

'Oh yes, lad. Mice, moths, woodlice, cockroaches. The odd rat, probably. It's a miniature zoo, this cupboard.'

Sammy didn't enjoy C.D.T. that afternoon. He couldn't concentrate. He kept picturing old Hannay in his blue and white striped apron, rooting through Parker's cupboard. When he glanced across at Jane he thought she looked unwell. He wondered how Mrs Brook was getting along, and when the boys did the rap at break he didn't join in.

On Wednesday, Jane and Sammy decided they wouldn't eat school lunch unless they knew what it was. Sammy said, 'How do we find out what it is?'

'We ask,' Jane told him. At eleven o'clock she stuck her hand up and asked to go to the toilet but went to the kitchen instead. Mr Hannay wasn't there, but Mrs Trafford was. 'Where's Mr Hannay?' asked Jane. She hoped he'd left, but Mrs Trafford said, 'He's just slipped along to the gym, dear. Why – who wants him?'

'Oh, nobody,' said Jane. 'I was wondering what's for dinner, that's all.'

'Opek,' said Mrs Trafford.

'Pardon?' said Jane.

'Opek. It's a very old oriental dish, Mr Hannay says. Very nice.'

Opek turned out to be a grey, porridgy mush. It didn't look all that promising, but it was probably what ancient oriental grub was supposed to look like, and it tasted fine. Everybody was enjoying it till Gaz Walker fished a small flat rectangular object from his plate and held it up.

'Here,' he complained. 'Why is there a Size 4 tag in my dinner?'

'Let's have a look.' Jane took the tag and examined it. It looked like the sort of tag you'd find inside a shoe. 'Opek,' she murmured, wondering why Mr Hannay had been in the gym when he was supposed to be cooking. 'Opek.' An idea formed in her head and sank slowly into her stomach where it lay like a lead weight. She put the tag on the rim of her plate and sat back with her hands across her stomach. All round the table, kids stopped eating and watched her.

'What's up, Jane?' Sammy's voice was husky.

'Opek,' whispered Jane. 'I think I know what it means.'

'What does it mean?' asked Jeannette, who had almost cleared her plate.

'I think it's initials,' said Jane. 'Standing for Old P.E. Kit.'

The peace of the dining area was shattered by cries of revulsion and the scrape and clatter of

70

chairs as everybody on Jane's table stampeded for the door. The kids at the other tables watched till they'd gone, then lowered their heads and went on eating opek.

Sometimes two people can keep a secret, but never ten. There were ten kids at Jane and Sammy's table, and so the secret came out. Nobody went into dinner on Thursday. Nobody. At twelve o'clock Mr Hannay raised the hatch and found himself gazing at twelve empty tables. He frowned at his watch. Shook it. Raised it to his ear. At five-past twelve he took off his apron and went to see the head. They stood at the head's window, looking towards the playing field. All the children were there, and some seemed to be eating the grass. 'Good lord,' sighed the head. 'What did you cook, Hannay?'

'Epsatsc,' said the chef.

'Never heard of it,' said the head. 'What is it?'

'Traditional Greek dish,' said Hannay smoothly, easily fooling the head. Jane, who'd got the word from Mrs Trafford, wasn't fooled. 'Epsatsc' she said, grimly, leaning on a goal post. 'Erasers, pencil shavings and the school cat.'

On Friday everybody brought sandwiches but they needn't have, because Hannay had gone and Mrs Brook was back. When they spotted her crossing the playground at five to nine the kids cheered. Mrs Brook, who was the sentimental type, had to wipe her eyes before she could see to hang up her coat. The kids chucked their butties in the bin and Sammy's rap was dead.

Dinner wasn't fish and chips, but there were no complaints. Everybody tucked in with gusto – even

Sammy. The snowy cloths had gone and there were no flowers, but there was something else instead. Contentment. You could feel it all around.

And so the school week drew to a close. Everybody relaxed. The work was done. The weekend, bright with promise, lay ahead. At half-past three the kids spilled whooping into the yard and away down the drive. Jane and Sammy, in no rush, strolled behind. At the top of the drive stood the gardener, looking lost. Sammy grinned. 'What's up, Mr Tench?' The gardener lifted his cap and scratched his head. 'Nay,' he growled. 'There were a pile of nice, fresh horse manure here this morning and it's gone.'

The twins exchanged glances. Mrs Brook was coming down the drive. They ran to her. 'Mrs Brook!' cried Sammy. 'That Mr Hannay – he has left, hasn't he?'

The cook nodded. 'Yes, dear, I'm afraid he has but don't worry – he left me his recipe book, and you know it's just amazing the meals you can get out of stuff you find lying around.'

Terrance Dicks

I was born in East London and grew up during the Second World War, the period in which this story is set. After passing my eleven-plus – just – I went to grammar school then on to Cambridge University. After my compulsory National Service in the army, I worked first in advertising and then as a radio and television scriptwriter. I was script-editor of Dr Who *for many years and later, first the script-editor then producer of the BBC Television's Classic Serial.*

Now a full-time writer, I've written over a hundred children's books and in a recent survey, I was very proud to be in the top ten most widely read children's writers along with Roald Dahl and Enid Blyton! One of my most recent books is Prisoners of War.

I am married and live in Hampstead in London with my wife, and three sons.

The Barrier

'It's no good, Tony,' said Jacko. 'This time we're doomed.'

Jacko was my best friend. We were with the rest of the gang in our secret underground hideout beneath war-battered London.

'Come off it,' I said, doing my best to sound brave. 'Don't give up now, we might still do all right.'

Jacko's little brother Tommy piped up. 'Yeah, there's always a chance.'

'They're not after you, are they?' said Fatty Harwood bitterly. 'You're too young. Your turn'll come.'

'They won't scare me,' said Tommy, who was a right little hard nut. But he looked worried all the same.

It wasn't the enemy bombers that had nearly flattened London that were striking such terror into our hearts. We'd all faced bombs cheerfully enough in our time.

It wasn't the invading Nazi hordes, Hitler's apparently invincible army that had once conquered Europe in what seemed like days. They'd never made it as far as England, and now they never would.

The war was over.

'We won the war, in 1944,' we used to sing. (We'd won in 1945 actually, but that didn't rhyme.)

Anyway, we won. Not without a bit of help from the Yanks and the Russians, mind you. Well, quite a lot of help to be honest. For us kids, peace was a bit of a let-down, all the same hardships without the excitement. Food was still rationed – bread rationing didn't even *start* until after the war. A few strange exotic delicacies had started appearing in the shops. Things some of us had never even seen before, like bananas for instance ...

And even though bombing was over the bomb sites were still there. Fenced-off areas of ruins and rubble that had once been buildings, they were the adventure playgrounds of our time. We knew all the good bomb sites in the area, me and my gang. The gang was me and Jacko, Jacko's little brother Tommy, and Fatty Harwood.

Tommy was really too young to be a proper member, but he was a tough little kid and we couldn't get rid of him.

'Who *found* the hideout then?' he'd say, whenever we told him to push off.

The hideout was under a bomb site just off the high street. Tommy was the one who found it, right enough, though not exactly on purpose. He was scrambling over the ruins one day and he just disappeared. Muffled yells of 'Help! Get me out!' came from somewhere underground.

We followed them and found a room preserved beneath the rubble. There was even some rotting furniture, an old couch, armchair and a table. 'I reckon the place must have been the caretaker's basement before a bomb flattened this place,' I said.

'Well, it's our hideout now,' said Jacko.

We always gathered in the hideout in times of danger.

We were down there that particular Saturday morning, discussing a menace that was worrying us a lot more than Hitler ever had. More even than the daily menace of our deadly rivals, Ginger Markham's gang, a collection of thugs who chased us round the bomb sites and heaved half bricks at us on sight.

This looming terror was called the eleven-plus.

Just after your eleventh birthday you took an exam – *the* exam, you might say. It decided which sort of school you went to – Grammar or Secondary Modern.

At Grammar School, you got a black blazer with a badge on, a cap with another badge on, a school tie and a long woolly scarf. Oh yes, and they threw in an education as well.

At the Secondary Modern they gave you a green blazer, taught you useful things like cookery and woodwork and tried to keep you off the streets till you were old enough to go out to work. Maybe that's not a fair picture but that's how most people saw it … They sorted you out early back in those days.

'Well, it's coming,' said Jacko. 'And it's coming next week. So unless we're going to hide down here forever … '

'Let's do that,' said Tommy, always one for a mad scheme. 'We could be outlaws, come out at night and steal food … '

It was a nice idea in its way, but even I could see it wasn't really practical. 'It's only another test,' I said. 'This time next week it'll be all over.'

The exam came round and we all staggered through it somehow. After that life went back to normal – till the results came through.

I'd passed – just.

Jacko and Fatty had both failed.

Jacko wasn't bothered, or so he said. 'Suits me fine. I'll be earning good money when you're still miserable little schoolkids, begging your mums for sixpence to go to the pictures.'

Fatty's failure was the big surprise – he was the brightest of the three of us.

'I was in such a panic I didn't know what I was doing,' he said miserably. 'When the exam started I had a job remembering my name, and I think I even spelt that wrong!'

Jacko came round unexpectedly a few nights later. I remember because it was the same day my mum had just bought all the Grammar School gear at the outfitters in the high street.

Blazer, grey shorts (we wore little grey shorts in the first year, believe it or not. Shorts – at eleven!), cap, scarf and tie, all laid out on a chair in my bedroom.

Jacko looked casually at it. 'This is the outfit then, is it?'

'Yeah, that's it,' I said. 'Look, let's go out, shall we?'

'Hang on a minute,' said Jacko. 'Mind if I try it on?'

'All right, if you like. It won't fit though.'

I was tall and skinny and Jacko was shorter and broader.

Jacko put on the blazer.

He looked at himself in my old bedroom mirror for a moment. Then he took the blazer off, and laid it carefully back on the chair. 'You're right, it doesn't fit. Let's find Fatty and Tommy and get up a game of rounders.' You played rounders, a sort of basic baseball, round four lampposts in the street.

'We can play outside Mrs Wilkins',' said Jacko. 'I bet she starts banging on the window at us again.' Mrs Wilkins was convinced one of us would break her windows one of these days.

We were in luck that afternoon. Old Mrs Wilkins came right out of her house waving her walking stick and chased us down the street …

There weren't many more street games for me and Jacko after that, not after we'd started at our different schools … We'd sworn it wouldn't make any difference but of course it did. We saw less and less of each other, and gradually the gang broke up altogether.

It wasn't easy, starting off at the bottom again in Grammar School. First-years were the lowest of the low. To begin with we were as good as gold and we stood up in class for everyone, teachers *and* prefects. There was a bit of mild, routine bullying from the years above us, but nothing too serious. After a bit we found our feet, and started standing up for ourselves, behaving, and misbehaving, like normal kids, shoving our caps in our pockets as soon as we got out of the school gates. It was taking a risk, though – you got a detention if a teacher saw you out without your cap.

'You're here to work!' the head told us when we

arrived. He was a terrifying figure in a flowing black gown, a mortarboard, and a big black bushy moustache. 'When the time comes, you will be expected to take – and pass – at least eight 'O' levels. If you stay on in the sixth form, as most boys do, you will take at least four 'A' levels. After that it will be time to think about university ... ' That's what we were expected to do, and that's exactly what most of us did – me included ...

I ran into Jacko once or twice in the next few years, but there was no way we could go on being friends. Green blazers and black were deadly enemies, and our sides had been chosen for us.

Fatty Harwood eventually came to join me at the Grammar. There was a second-chance entry at age fourteen, and a handful made it through the barrier. Not Jacko, though. He was already into another kind of life as I was soon to find out.

I was cycling home latish one night after a rehearsal for the school play. I was playing Bassanio in *The Merchant of Venice* - not that big a part, but there were a few good lines in it and I'd insisted on wearing a big bushy moustache like the head's which was good for a laugh in itself.

Fatty, who'd developed into quite an actor, was playing Shylock. I was having trouble with a wonky front lamp which was off more than it was on. It was off as I took my usual short cut down a dark alley behind some shops. Suddenly, I rode bang into the middle of a group of shadowy figures carrying cartons. I went down with a noisy crash, and so did most of the figures. There were yells of pain and anger, someone fell noisily over a pile of tin dustbins, lights went on near by, and someone else yelled, 'Scarper!'

It was my old enemy Ginger Markham, clutching a big cardboard carton of cigarettes.

He shoved his way past me and disappeared down the end of the alley. Someone else trampled over me and I struggled to my feet in time to confront the last member of the gang.

It was Jacko. I think he was as amazed as I was.

For a moment we just looked at each other. Then there were shouts from the end of the alley and the sound of a police whistle.

Jacko made to dash past me but I blocked his way. Jacko looked hard at me. 'Get out of my way, Tone.'

'Not that way, you idiot,' I said. 'Over the wall and through the back gardens.'

'Give us a leg-up!'

Jacko made a scrambling leap for the top of the high stone wall, and I gave him a shove that sent him right over the other side. I heard the thump of his landing, and then the sound of footsteps moving away.

It wasn't much of a reunion.

Then there were more footsteps, heavy-booted ones coming down the alley. A torch shone in my face and the voice of the Law said its classic line.

'Now then, what's going on?'

I had a bit of trouble with the policeman.

'You were the lookout, were you? Didn't I see you helping one of them get away?'

I managed to talk my way out of trouble – just. I told him my name, where I'd been, where I lived, and that the alley was a short cut between school and home that I'd often used before. I told him how I'd crashed into the figures in the alley and we'd all come a cropper.

All perfectly true.

After that the story got a bit dodgy.

'I was trying to catch that last one, officer,' I said, doing my best to sound like one of dear old Enid's *Famous Five*. 'He got away from me over the wall.'

I think the copper was still a bit suspicious, but my battered appearance and bashed-up bike supported my story.

'All right, son, off you go,' said the policeman. 'And see you do something about that wonky front lamp.'

I was about to push my bike away – the front wheel was buckled – when he said, 'Just a minute, sonny.'

I waited.

'Those kids were all about your age. Didn't recognise any of them, did you?'

'Sorry, it all happened too fast.'

He sighed, but he must have been used to it. Nobody told the coppers much round our way. 'All right, clear off.'

I shoved the bike away.

I hadn't done old Jacko much of a favour really.

A few months later Dad passed me the local paper. 'One of your old mates seems to be in trouble.'

Jacko had been caught robbing an off-licence. It wasn't his first offence by a long way and they sent him away to some kind of Borstal.*

* *Corrective establishment for young offenders.*

'He'll get an education there all right,' said my dad grimly. 'From all the other little villains.'

That was the last I ever heard of my one-time best friend Jacko, but I still think about him now and again.

About the time he came round and tried on my blazer and took it off again, and an invisible barrier came down between us.

A barrier that meant I was classed as clever, and could pass exams and get a good job.

A barrier that must have made Jacko feel he was second-rate, a reject, who might as well grab all he could get.

A barrier that sorted out my life and Jacko's too – when we were eleven years old.

Vivien Alcock

I was born in Worthing, Sussex, the youngest of three sisters. We were seaside children, with sand between our toes and our rooms filled with drying seaweed and shells and coloured pebbles. In summer, we played for hours on the beach. In winter, we would dress up in mackintoshes, sou'westers and gumboots and go and watch the waves crashing against the sea wall, throwing up fountains of spray high above our heads.

Our mother was ill for as long as I can remember, and I think this drew the three of us closer together. We were all fond of painting and reading, and used to tell each other bedtime stories. As I was the youngest, my turn came last, and before I had properly begun, my sisters would be fast asleep. Even the cat would be asleep. I think this is what made me want to be a writer. I was determined to get my stories told at last.

For some reason, before I was twelve, we kept changing schools. This meant we were often new girls, coming into our different classes where everyone else had been together for ages – always apt to be difficult if you're shy. Sometimes the teacher would ask someone to look after us for the first day or two. Sometimes we were left to sink or swim. I only once came across a school bully, in a school whose name I have happily forgotten. She didn't think much of me. She told me so the first day. 'I don't like you,' she said, just like that, out of the blue. I was miserable there, until one day, like the girl in my story, I received a gift of flowers, and realised that someone, somewhere, did like me.

After school, I studied at the Oxford School of Art, intending to be a teacher, but I volunteered for the army before I had finished my course. This was at the time of the Second World War, and things were going badly for us. I can't pretend my joining the army made the slightest difference to the course of the war, but it made an enormous difference to me! I was an ambulance driver, serving in France, Belgium and Germany. My husband, Leon Garfield, was in the Medical Corps, and we met in an army canteen in Belgium. He too wanted to be either an artist or a writer. As it happened he became a writer long before I did.

After the war, I worked as a commercial artist for several years, only stopping when our daughter Jane was born. Telling her bedtime stories awakened my interest in writing again and that is how I began.

Vivien Alcock's most recent novels are A Kind of Thief *and* The Trial of Anna Cotman.

Flowers for the New Girl

Barbara Heston is the most important person in our class. She is a large girl with a loud voice, curly red hair and big white teeth. Her friends say she is pretty. If you're small, you keep out of her way.

The new girl was small. Her name was Lily Barnes, though she looked more like a weed than a lily, being thin and nervous, as if she was afraid some gardener would come and yank her out by the roots and throw her on the rubbish heap. She was wearing the wrong clothes.

Our school doesn't have a uniform. We wear what we choose – or rather what Barbara chooses, for we all try to copy her. Her parents are rich, and she always wears the latest and most expensive fashions, which we follow as best we can. This term it was sleeveless blouses, miniskirts and ankle socks, though it was a cold May and our arms and legs became blue and goose-pimpled, and the boys jeered at us. Lily came to school wearing shabby grey trousers with a patch on one knee, a red and green jumper too small for her and white trainers. I saw Barbara look her up and down and wrinkle her nose like at a bad smell.

One of Barbara's friends said something to her and they both laughed. They began calling the new girl 'Jumble', I suppose because she looked as if she'd got her clothes from a jumble sale. It caught on. We all began to call the new girl Jumble, and soon it was as if she'd never had another name. She didn't ask us not to, but I know she minded. Her eyes often looked glossy and when she saw me watching her, she'd turn her head away. I'm sure she was close to tears.

One day she did cry. Barbara lost a pound coin out of the pocket of her cardigan, which she had hung over the back of her chair in the canteen. She said somebody must have stolen it while she and her friends were queuing for their sausage and chips. She looked straight at Jumble when she said this, so of course we all looked at Jumble, too. Jumble who was sitting alone at the next table. Jumble who was poor.

'It wasn't me,' she said, but she flushed scarlet and her eyes looked glossy again, and everybody thought she was guilty.

'Give it back to me,' Barbara said, holding out her hand. 'Give it back right now, or you'll be sorry. You'll wish you'd never been born.'

'I haven't got it!' Jumble cried, and now her tears spilled over. 'I never touched your cardigan!'

'Let's search her,' somebody said.

We all moved towards her and she fled, out of the canteen and down the corridor, running like a terrified mouse looking for a dark hole to hide in. We went whooping after her, but Miss Greenleigh, coming out of the art room, stopped us.

'What do you think you're doing?' she demanded. 'You know you're not supposed to run in the corridors. Barbara, what's going on?'

'Nothing,' Barbara said automatically. 'We were just playing tag.'

'Well, go and play it in the playground,' Miss Greenleigh said. 'That's what playgrounds are for. And go quietly.'

So Jumble got away. She wasn't in the playground. She must have found a dark hole somewhere safe. Just before we went in again, I saw Barbara pull her hanky out of the pocket of her skirt. Something fell on to the ground and spun for a moment in the sunlight. It was her pound coin. Barbara picked it up and made a face and said something to her friend. They both giggled. 'Oh well,' Barbara said. 'I bet she does pinch things. Did you see how guilty she looked?'

'Are you going to tell her you found it?' her friend asked.

'I suppose I'll have to,' Barbara said reluctantly.

I watched her that afternoon. She never went near Jumble. She didn't pass her a note. She didn't even look at her. When the final bell went, Jumble left quickly, as she always did, flying from the school like an escaped prisoner. If I hadn't been good at running, I'd never have caught her. When I put my hand on her arm, she shrieked.

'It's only me,' I said, 'I thought I'd tell you – Barbara found her pound. It was in the pocket of her skirt, not her cardigan, after all. She – ' I hesitated, not wanting to say anything against Barbara in case it got back to her. I didn't want to find myself an outcast, too. So I changed it to – 'She would have told you but you went off so quickly. So I thought I'd tell you.'

'Thank you,' she said, staring at me as if she'd

never seen me before, like I was some sort of unexpected angel. But she must've known me because she said my name, 'Thank you, Bess.'

'Think nothing of it, Lily,' I said, and ran off quickly. I was afraid to be friends with her, afraid someone would see us together and tell Barbara. I'm not one of those who think Barbara Heston is pretty. I can too easily imagine those big white teeth crunching bones. My bones, if I wasn't careful. So I ran off and left Jumble staring after me.

The next morning, when we went into our classroom, there was a great pile of purple lilac heaped on Miss Greenleigh's desk and, on the blackboard behind it, written in neat, sloping handwriting, this message –

Flowers for the New Girl.

'That's Lily Barnes,' Miss Greenleigh said. 'She's the only new girl this term. Lily? Where is she?'

Jumble came forward slowly, almost as if expecting to be told off. But Miss Greenleigh had a soft spot for her. I think she guessed we were giving her a bad time. 'Here you are, Lily,' she said kindly. 'If you take them to the art room, I expect Miss Porter will give you something to put them in until you go home. Tell her I sent you.'

'Thank you,' Jumble whispered.

The lilac filled her arms. The purple flowers, nestling like tiny bunches of blue grapes in the soft green foliage, gave off a warm, sweet scent. When she turned to leave the room, I saw her small face framed in leaves. She was looking at me, her eyes shining with wonder and delight. She smiled and I realised that she thought the flowers were from me. I shook my head.

'Who put them there?' Miss Greenleigh asked. We all looked at one another but nobody spoke.

'Apparently Lily has a secret friend,' Miss Greenleigh said. 'It was a kind thought, but please, another time, not on my desk. Bess, will you clean the blackboard while I get the books out?'

Flowers for the New Girl. The writing was neat and regular, all the loops sloping the same way. Nothing like mine – as I pointed out to Barbara and her friends in the playground later, when they came crowding around me. They seemed to think I had done it, though I swore I hadn't. 'Honest-to-God,' I said, hopping about on one leg.

'Well, who was it then?' Barbara demanded.

I suggested it might have been one of the boys, but nobody believed this. The boys in our class are not a romantic lot. They think of nothing but football and cars. Besides, as Barbara remarked, who on earth could feel romantic about Jumble? I think it was this that made her so angry, the fact that Jumble got the flowers, not her. It didn't take her long to find a way to spoil it.

'I bet she put them there herself,' she said. 'Did you notice it wasn't a proper bunch, not tied up or wrapped in paper. If you ask me, she got them from that old bush behind the cycle shed.'

We all trooped off to have a look. Sure enough, there was evidence that the bush had been robbed. Some of the thin branches were broken off, the fresh breaks showing white in the sunlight, and there were leaves and twigs on the ground.

'She's stolen our school lilac!' Barbara cried indignantly. 'What cheek. She must've come very early and put them on the desk herself, and then sneaked out again so that she could come back later, pretending to be surprised. I always knew she was a thief.'

'A bit of old lilac – we don't even know she did it,' I said. 'Why should she give herself flowers? It doesn't make sense.'

'She wanted to feel important, of course,' Barbara said. 'Come on, let's find her and make her say sorry.'

So we all went off to find Jumble – I don't know why I keep saying 'we'. I'm not really one of them. I wanted to be once, but not any longer. I just hang about on the edge of things, worrying, not knowing what to do. I wish I was braver. But luckily they didn't find Jumble. She'd gone to the dentist.

On Monday morning, there was another message on the blackboard. No flowers this time, just the message in the same sloping handwriting –

Leave the new girl alone, you smelly bullies, or you'll be sorry.

Barbara rubbed it off quickly before Miss Greenleigh arrived. She was mad. Her face was crimson, clashing with her curly red hair, and her teeth looked bigger than ever.

'She's the one who'll be sorry,' she said.

She was convinced that Jumble had done it and was hiding somewhere.

'It's nothing like her writing,' I said quickly. 'Honest, I'm sure it wasn't her.'

90

She turned her hot blue eyes towards me and they didn't seem to like what they saw. 'Perhaps you did it yourself,' she said.

'No! I didn't! I didn't! Cross my heart,' I squealed. She frightens me. She walks through my nightmares at night, grinding her teeth.

'Bess wouldn't have the nerve,' a girl called Sharon said. To my surprise she winked at me with the eye that Barbara could not see.

'If it wasn't her, who was it then?' Barbara demanded angrily.

'Perhaps it was a ghost,' somebody said.

'Why don't you ask it?' Sharon suggested. 'Write a letter on the blackboard after school. Ask who it thinks it is.'

We all laughed. That was what Barbara was fond of saying to anyone who disagreed with her. 'Who do you think you are?' she'd demand, coming up close to them.

'All right, I will,' she said, tossing her head; and she did. We hung about until the last bell had gone and everyone else, including Jumble, had left. Then she wrote on the blackboard –

Are you scared to sign your name, you miserable little worm? I am not. I am Barbara Heston and I warn you. When I find you, you'll wish you were dead.

We read it in silence. Then Sharon said, 'That's hardly going to encourage anybody to own up. You'd better come to school early tomorrow and wipe it off before old Greenleigh sees it, or you'll be in trouble.'

'Oh, I'll be here early,' Barbara said, showing her big teeth. 'We'll see if the little worm comes out of her hole.' I knew she still thought it was Jumble; Jumble who had run off, as usual, as soon as the last bell rang. 'There'll be no more messages after this,' she said confidently.

She was right, I thought. No more messages. It would all be as it had been before, with everyone agreeing with Barbara and poor Jumble out in the cold, creeping about with nightmares in her eyes. No more lilac to make her smile at the thought that she had a friend somewhere.

You see, I was the worm who was afraid to come out of her hole. In spite of my swearing honest-to-God and crossing my heart like it was a Good Friday bun, it had been me who'd picked the school lilac from behind the cycle shed. Me who'd written the two messages on the blackboard in a carefully disguised hand. I had wanted to help Lily secretly, but it hadn't done her any good. If anything it had made things worse for her. There would be no more messages on the blackboard.

I was wrong. When I got to school the next morning, Barbara and her friends were already there, staring at the board. I stared too. I think my face must have gone as white as chalk, for there it was, written in the same sloping handwriting that I had used –

I am Liza. You cannot frighten me. I am already dead. Tomorrow I will come and fetch you away. Barbara, say goodbye to your friends.

I didn't blame Barbara for looking like curdled cream.

'What rubbish!' she said loudly, looking round at us suspiciously, wondering which of us had done it, who had dared. Liza? There wasn't a Liza in our school. We didn't know any Liza. Barbara stared at me with her boiled blue eyes. Liza is short for Elizabeth, and so is Bess. But it wasn't me. Nobody's ever called me Liza. I've always been Bess. Ask anyone.

Barbara told me to clean the blackboard and be sharp about it, before Miss Greenleigh arrived. I wiped it hastily with the duster, smudging the white chalk, seeing the name Liza disappear slowly, dust unto dust.

'Hurry up,' Barbara said.

I rubbed harder. The smell of the chalk was thick in my nose. The boys started coming in, chatting and pushing each other. 'What are you doing?' Tom Hatch asked me. I didn't answer but went on rubbing. I couldn't get all the writing out. 'You need a damp sponge,' Tom advised me, but it was too late. Miss Greenleigh was coming. I dropped the duster and ran back to my table. On the blackboard, I could still see very faintly, like the ghosts of words – *say goodbye to your friends*.

I glanced at Barbara and saw that she was staring at it too. Then she turned and glared at me. She thought I'd left it there on purpose. When the bell rang, she took me by the arm and marched me out into the playground. Some girls were standing, looking down.

'Hey, Barbara,' one of them called. 'Here's another message.'

It was written in chalk, the letters printed and very large –

TOMORROW I WILL COME AND TAKE YOU AWAY.

'Who did that?' Barbara shouted, dropping my

arm, forgetting about me. 'Who did it?' She looked round at her friends. 'It was one of you,' she accused, but they all shook their heads.

'It must have been the school ghost,' one of them said.

'A girl called Liza hanged herself on the lilac tree behind the bicycle shed ages ago,' a second one joined in.

'Because she'd been bullied,' said a third.

I'd never heard of this before. Perhaps they were making it up. I could see some of them smiling. Barbara didn't smile. She started rubbing the words off the concrete with her feet, standing with her head lowered, pawing the ground like a large red bull.

But she could not rub all the messages out. They came thick and fast now, chalked on the school walls, written on blackboards, on her table in the canteen – *My name is Liza. I am already dead. Liza. Liza. Tomorrow I will come and fetch you away. Say goodbye to your friends.*

I never thought I would feel sorry for Barbara Heston but I did. She seemed to dwindle before our eyes. Jumble and I sat together in the art room. We couldn't help watching her. It was like seeing ice melt away in the hot sun. She was sitting there, crying on to her painting, making the colours run like blood.

'What's the matter with her?' Lily asked. She had come in too late this morning to see the new message on the blackboard. I told her about it.

'And now they're everywhere. Look!'

I pointed. The window was clouded over with condensation, and on the misty surface, somebody had written with a clean finger, *Barbara Heston, say goodbye to your friends*. I wiped it off with my hand.

'Do you think Liza is a ghost?' Lily whispered.

'I don't know.'

Tom Hatch and his friends were whispering and giggling together, not that there was anything unusual in that. I remembered Tom watching me as I wiped the message off the blackboard this morning, and wondered how long he'd been there. I got up, pretending I wanted to sharpen my pencil. When I passed their table, I stopped and said, 'Is this your doing, Tom?'

'What? What are you talking about?'

'These new messages.'

'What messages?'

His face was as innocent as a newborn lamb's, and his brain as woolly. I didn't really think it could be him. He wasn't sharp enough to have thought of it. I went back to my place.

Miss Porter had noticed that Barbara was crying. She went over to her and began talking to her quietly. Barbara put her head down on her wet painting and sobbed. We were all quiet then, looking at each other with guilty eyes. Miss Porter led Barbara out of the room.

She never came back. Her parents sent her to a posh boarding school in Sussex. We saw her sometimes in the holidays, walking along with new friends, dressed in the very latest fashions. We don't miss her. Even her old friends seem happier now she's gone, and Lily and I can't believe our luck.

We never found out who chalked the Liza messages all over the school that day. Nobody ever owned up. Nor can we remember who started the story about the ghost who hanged herself from the lilac tree. Miss Porter, who's been here since the school first opened, says it's nonsense. It's hardly a thing she's likely to have forgotten, is it? she asks. I suppose not. But we don't like to go near the lilac tree by ourselves, not in winter when it gets dark early. All except Lily, who is surprisingly brave, but that is only because she still believes it was me all the time. How could it have been? I've only one pair of hands.

Robert Westall

I loved school – all my schools. My three great passions were English, art and rugby football. I was a thin clumsy child, then when I was eleven, the Second World War broke out and my mother made it her duty to see I didn't starve to death (as she had almost done in the previous war owing to the U-boat blockades). By twelve, I was an enormous, clumsy child then miraculously at fifteen, the fat disappeared and employing intelligence as well as mountainous strength, I not only got my school colours, I reached the County All Age Final trials. It was always a toss-up whether I actually caught the ball or not – I found it easier to catch and flatten the people who did have the ball!

I eventually became a teacher and taught art in a sixth-form college for twenty-eight years. I couldn't stand art after four o'clock so turned to writing for a hobby. Had I taught English, no doubt I would now be a weekend painter. Funny how life works out.

I've owned sixty-seven cats since 1957. Cats to me are one of life's great and certain plusses. My favourite cat is Geoffrey, who is very small and has silver and pink fur. He has inspired two of my books – A Walk on the Wild Side *and* If Cats Could

Fly in which spacemen give him the power to think and fly!

I have written two books for adults but have no desire to write any more. It is writing for the young that turns me on. I don't feel I have changed much inside since I was sixteen and I'm rather glad. Sixteen thinks deeply and feels as dark as doom then can suddenly switch to being a cheerful animal playing tennis or climbing mountains.

Sixteen can stay up all night at a party, eat a hearty breakfast and go off playing rugby. Sixteen is incredibly nosy and openminded. At least I am still incredibly nosy and openminded. But I miss the tennis and the rugby and the mountaineering and hurling my body about like a lunatic and never feeling a twinge.

Perhaps my books for the young still make it possible for me to do these things – in my mind.

The White Cat

Of course you all knew Kay Kingsley, the intrepid TV reporter. Kay who cycled round Bucharest with her camera crew while the Securitate were still shooting students. Kay whom President Reagan called 'sweetie-pie' at a press conference. (Much good it did him.) Kay whom Mr Gorbachev always had a smile for, no matter how bad his crises.

All my grown-up life I seem to have been seeing her, microphone in hand, against a sea of flaming vehicles. With her big blue eyes squinted up, and that tigerish grin of glee on her face. But there's one thing I always noticed about her, that perhaps you haven't. She always wore a little white badge on her spotted combat-jacket. And if you looked closely enough, you'd see the badge is a little white enamel cat.

I, and only I, know why she wore it. Because I was there at her beginning. At Umpleby Grammar School. I was her boyfriend. Well, sort of. More her ever-willing slave, perhaps.

We were sitting at the same table during double maths; the maths teacher was called Ellis the Trellis, because everyone saw through him so easily. I was sitting next to her, ever-eager to do her bidding. It was the top maths set, because she was a bright spark even then. So was I, in those days, even though I later became a chartered accountant.

Anyway, on this particular day, I noticed she was staring at the ceiling. Mind you, we all stared at the ceiling during double maths in search of inspiration, solace, or merely escape. But usually everybody else's eyes were out of focus. Kay's, however, on this occasion, were as sharp as needles. She was actually *watching* something.

I followed her eye, to see what she was staring at. There were the usual damp stains on the ceiling, that looked like maps of South Island New Zealand, or Tierra del Fuego. The only other thing was a hatch in the ceiling, a wire grille set in a surround of shiny brown wood, about as exciting as having your hair cut. But it was that that she was staring at. With great intentness.

'What's up wi' you?' I hissed. I was afraid that the boredom of Ellis the Trelllis's lessons had finally driven her nuts. I was scared that one of the other lads would notice, and nobody likes their girlfriend being called nuts. I mean, you might have to bash somebody for it. Even someone bigger than yourself.

'There's something up there,' she whispered. 'Behind the grille. Something white. It keeps on coming and going.'

'Bit of waste paper,' I hissed, 'blowing in the draught.'

'No,' she said. 'It's *watching* me.'

I broke out in a cold sweat. Ellis the Trellis must have really blown her mind this time. I contemplated the third-year equivalent of divorce, which was sitting at somebody else's table.

Anyway, just then the bell went; and Ellis the Trellis fled to the staff room before we lynched him, and the rest of the set went after him like the usual herd of elephants.

'C'mon,' I said gruffly, to distract her. 'Let's go to the tuck shop. I'll buy you a Mars Bar.' I was down to my last thirty p, but love is love.

'No,' she said, putting her chair on the table beneath the hatch in the ceiling. 'I'm going to find out what it is.' She got up on the chair, and pushed at the hatch. It moved, revealing darkness. And then, of all things, the head of a small white cat peered down at her, ears pricked.

I was so glad she wasn't crazy.

The cat sniffed her fingers, tentatively. Then, when she tried to grab it, it moved back into the darkness like greased lightning, the way cats do.

'I'm going up after it,' she said. 'It might be trapped up there. It might be *starving*.'

'For God's sake,' I said. 'It's nearly bell-time. We're due in N14 for geography. We can report it to the caretaker.'

'No,' she said. 'He might take it to be put down or anything. I'm going up.' And she put her hands round the edge of the hatch and heaved herself halfway through.

And then the bell went. She was stuck.

'Help me, Stan,' came her muffled plea. 'Push my bum.'

I pushed – and she vanished with a last sexy wriggle which I still remember to this day.

I whipped the grille cover back in place just as

the Fifth came piling in, led by Mr Jameson, the history master, who did not like me. And there I was, standing alone with my head against the ceiling.

'Ho,' says Jameson. 'There you are, Timpson! Practising to join the circus? You should have a good career there. As one of the performing baboons no doubt!'

The fifth year loved that.

Well, I got through double geography somehow. Even managed to keep a straight face and tell the geography teacher that Kay was lying down in the girl's sick room with a bad headache; the one place where every man fears to go. He got his own back by giving me fifty lines for not paying attention. Not paying attention? Crikey, I was going mad. She might asphyxiate up there, or come crashing through the plaster ceiling and break a leg.

Never was I so grateful to hear the school bell for the end of the day. I dashed back to the maths room. There wasn't a sound from the hatch.

'Come down for God's sake!' I bellowed at the ceiling.

I waited for nearly an hour and a half, nearly at my wit's end, convinced that she was dead.

It was at this point that Kay Kingsley walked in through the *door,* dusty as hell and grinning her head off.

'What the … why the … ?'

'Don't have a fit,' she said, 'come and have a Coke. I'm buying.'

She swung her legs sitting on the wall outside the newsagent's and pulled the ring off her Coke can.

'I came down through the hatch in the girls' toilets,' she said cheerfully. 'Seemed the safest place. The roof space all joins up, and there's a hatch in the ceiling of every room. Must be a ventilation system.'

'But what took you so *long?*'

'Oh, Stan, it was so *fascinating* up there. I couldn't tear myself away.'

'Oh, very fascinating, I'm sure,' I said sarcastically. 'Spiders and cobwebs, dust and dead flies. What do you want to be when you grow up? The Mummy's Curse?'

'Well, there was the cat. Though she wouldn't let me catch her, and soon shot off, through a broken ventilator in the wall over the bike sheds. I never saw her again.'

'So ... ?'

'Well, you can look down into all the rooms, and watch people without being seen, and hear what they are saying. Did you know the head practises putting with a golf club in his study? Into the waste basket? And talks to himself while he's doing it, pretending to be Nick Faldo?'

That pinned my ears back.

'And I think Mr Chambers and Miss Ramsden are in *love*. They stayed in the staff room after the rest had left, and were holding hands and whispering sweet nothings to each other.'

'But Mr Chambers is married. His wife and kids came to Sports Day ... '

'The secrets of all hearts shall be revealed,' she said, with a wink. 'I'm going to start a gossip column in the school newspaper.'

The school newspaper was a crummy inky thing run by a bunch of sixth formers. In a school of eight hundred, it sold about fifty copies, because people just borrowed it off those foolish enough to actually buy it. I mean, it cost the price of half a Mars bar. But the moment Kay's Kolumn, as it was called, began to be published, the circulation trebled. She spent a lot of time up in the roof space, though now she used the hatch in the girls' toilets most of the time, which kept me out of it.

She never overplayed her hand; but she got some rare scoops. She forecast the parents were going to buy us a swimming bath; and it happened. She was the first with the news that Rogerson had been chosen to play in the North of England trials at rugby. She gave us the news that Mr Chambers and Miss Ramsden were going to organise a long school trip to the Loire Valley Châteaux next summer. Mr Chambers and Miss Ramsden walked around the school looking very pale and sweaty for days, and she said they gave her very funny looks ...

But she never overplayed her hand. She always started off any forecast with her famous phrase 'rumour hath it that'. And the staff, who were very put out at having so much of their business known, just thought that other members of staff had opened their big mouths too much too soon.

Until the fatal day that she came to me absolutely boiling over with rage and indignation.

'I've just heard the head talking to Rodney Tillotson's father on the phone. The head's going to make Rodney Tillotson head boy next year, because Father Tillotson's promised him a thousand quid for the minibus fund.'

'But Tillotson's a *weed*,' I said. 'He'll never get a grip. The school will be a *shambles*. There'll be riots!'

'I know,' she said, and that was when I first saw her eyes form those famous slits, and her face adopt that famous tigerish grin. 'And I'm going to stop it. And I need your help. I can't do it alone.'

'Why me?' I stammered, suddenly utterly terrified.

'I've got to get it into the school newspaper,' she said. 'Without the sixth-form editors reading it first. Without *anybody* reading it first.'

'How can you do that?'

'This fortnight's paper is lying in the school office, ready for duplicating … '

'And … ?'

'We're going to have to burgle the school after dark. We can climb up on the bike-shed roof and get into the roof space through that broken ventilator. The way the white cat gets in. Then we drop down into the secretary's office … It'll be as easy as pie … but you'll have to be there, to give me a leg up afterwards. Then I can pull you up after me.'

I nearly had a fit. But Kay could get a look of contempt on her face and I knew that if I refused, I'd be out in the cold for good. And besides, Rodney Tillotson was *such* a weed, and I admired Ben Scott, who should have been made head boy, or so everybody thought …

'OK,' I said.

'Tonight,' she said, with her tiger-look. 'Meet you at half-past seven at the youth club.'

I was glad it was that night. If I'd had to wait longer, I'm sure I'd have jumped in the river.

As it turned out, it was fatally easy. Nobody saw us go up over the bike-shed roof, or through the broken ventilator. And she knew her way by feel through the roof space, though I almost put my foot through a couple of ceilings, in my nervousness. But I shall never forget the moment when we got the grille off the hatch in the secretary's office, and I shone down my pencil-torch into the holy of holies.

'It looks so different from up here … ' I muttered.

'Everything looks so different from up here,' she said. 'I haven't seen the world the same at all, since the white cat first showed me all this. Everything in the world has got a polite face, that they show you down *there.* And everything's got another face, when you peep from up here. The things I've heard the men staff say about me … '

That made me mad then; that the men staff should talk about her so, even if she did have a smashing figure for her age, the best in the third year. And that rage gave me the courage to jump down, on to the secretary's desk.

It didn't take long. She riffled through the pages of the typed-up newspaper, and soon found a little gap at the bottom of a page. She shoved it into the secretary's typewriter and typed:

THE HEAD IS GOING TO MAKE RODNEY TILLOTSON HEAD BOY NEXT YEAR. TILLOT-

SON'S FATHER IS GIVING A THOUSAND POUNDS TO THE MINIBUS FUND.

And then she put the sheets back as they had been, ready for the photocopier. The sentence just looked like all the other typing. The secretary would never notice. The sixth formers stapling-up the sheets would never notice. Nobody would, until they read it.

Then we went back the way we came. Nobody saw us at all. We went back to the youth club, to give ourselves an alibi. And to drink Coke and dance. She danced for me alone that night. On her doorstep, she kissed me. I walked home, my feet hardly touched the ground.

Rodney Tillotson never made head boy. And they didn't get that thousand quid for the mini-bus fund. But teachers are not fools, whatever you say. They found the faint imprint of my trainers on the school secretary's blotting-pad. And they looked up and saw our dusty fingerprints on the shiny wooden surround of the ceiling grille. And then they found our footprints in the dust in the roof space.

Or rather the prints of *my* trainers, to be precise. For my dad had bought me them on our camping trip to France, and the patterns on the soles were like no others in the school.

And then Jameson must have told them about finding me doing my circus act under the grille in the maths room ...

I was on the head's carpet, and there were about five of them staring at me like I was a Nazi war criminal. And it wasn't just a matter of being expelled. There was talk of charges of burglary, and charges of criminal libel. And I was close to tears, thinking what it would do to my parents when they heard …

And then in bounced Kay, with that tigerish look set so hard on her face that I don't think it ever really came off ever again. And she started on about the things she'd seen from her roof space, and the things she'd heard. She really gave it to them … she'd hardly started when I was sent out of the room. I suppose they thought the things weren't fit for my ears.

She didn't come out of there until the bell went for home time. Then she just jerked her head at me and said, 'C'mon, let's get out of here. I'll buy you a Coke.'

We went and sat in the park, where it was peaceful. She swung her legs in triumph, and said, 'You're off the hook, Stan. You are merely the innocent dupe, led on by a wicked scheming young hussy. I'm the ringleader. It's only the ringleaders they ever really want. You just go back to school tomorrow, and keep your mouth shut, and you won't hear any more about it.'

'But you … ?'

'There are plenty of other schools. My father can afford to pay for a private one, where they'll take anybody if you pay enough. He'll probably send me off to a boarding school, as far away as possible.'

'Shan't … shan't I ever see you again?'

'Better not, Stan. For you, I'm *trouble.*'

'I wish I was like you, Kay.'

'But you're not, Stan. If you can't stand the heat,

stay out of the kitchen ... be a chartered accountant or something.'

'But shan't I *ever* see you again?' I wasn't just
saying goodbye to my first love; it was like saying
goodbye to a goddess ...

She smiled. 'Oh, I think you'll see me again. If
you go on watching the news long enough. There's
two sides to this world. The front side and the back
side. I'm going to show the world it's own back side
... There's nothing else I can do now. Since that
little white cat showed me the back side, I can't
look at anything else. I'm doomed, Stan, *doomed.'*

And with a wave of the hand, she was gone out
of my life forever.

Except, I watched the news for her. And, ten
years later, there she was in Belfast, against her
favourite backdrop of burning cars. Digging away
at the RUC's shoot-to-kill policy.

That was when I sent her the little white cat
badge ... which she always wore on her combat-
jacket after that. She sent me a handmade badge
in return; it must have cost her a packet.

The sole of a trainer; in red and gold.

Last week, as you know, she copped it in Beirut;
a sniper's bullet, in some stupid little square full of
wrecked concrete buildings. Still digging for the
truth. Doomed, as she said herself.

They say she was buried wearing the white cat;
nobody knew where the famous white cat had
come from.

Except me.

ALSO IN

Founding Editors: Anne and Ian Serraillier

Chinua Achebe Things Fall Apart
Douglas Adams The Hitchhiker's Guide to the Galaxy
Vivien Alcock The Cuckoo Sister; The Monster Garden; The
Trial of Anna Cotman; A Kind of Thief
Margaret Atwood The Handmaid's Tale
J G Ballard Empire of the Sun
Nina Bawden The Witch's Daughter; A Handful of Thieves;
Carrie's War; The Robbers; Devil by the Sea; Kept in the Dark;
The Finding; Keeping Henry; Humbug
E R Braithwaite To Sir, With Love
John Branfield The Day I Shot My Dad
F Hodgson Burnett The Secret Garden
Ray Bradbury The Golden Apples of the Sun; The Illustrated
Man
Betsy Byars The Midnight Fox; Goodbye, Chicken Little; The
Pinballs
Victor Canning The Runaways; Flight of the Grey Goose
Ann Coburn Welcome to the Real World
Hannah Cole Bring in the Spring
Jane Leslie Conly Racso and the Rats of NIMH
Robert Cormier We All Fall Down
Roald Dahl Danny, The Champion of the World; The Wonderful
Story of Henry Sugar; George's Marvellous Medicine; The BFG;
The Witches; Boy; Going Solo; Charlie and the Chocolate
Factory; Matilda
Anita Desai The Village by the Sea
Charles Dickens A Christmas Carol; Great Expectations
Peter Dickinson The Gift; Annerton Pit; Healer
Berlie Doherty Granny was a Buffer Girl
Gerald Durrell My Family and Other Animals
J M Falkner Moonfleet
Anne Fine The Granny Project
Anne Frank The Diary of Anne Frank
Leon Garfield Six Apprentices
Jamila Gavin The Wheel of Surya
Adele Geras Snapshots of Paradise

Graham Greene The Third Man and The Fallen Idol; Brighton Rock
Thomas Hardy The Withered Arm and Other Wessex Tales
Rosemary Harris Zed
L P Hartley The Go-Between
Ernest Hemingway The Old Man and the Sea; A Farewell to Arms
Nat Hentoff Does this School have Capital Punishment?
Nigel Hinton Getting Free; Buddy; Buddy's Song
Minfong Ho Rice Without Rain
Anne Holm I Am David
Janni Howker Badger on the Barge; Isaac Campion
Linda Hoy Your Friend Rebecca
Barbara Ireson (Editor) In a Class of Their Own
Jennifer Johnston Shadows on Our Skin
Toeckey Jones Go Well, Stay Well
James Joyce A Portrait of the Artist as a Young Man
Geraldine Kaye Comfort Herself; A Breath of Fresh Air
Clive King Me and My Million
Dick King-Smith The Sheep-Pig
Daniel Keyes Flowers for Algernon
Elizabeth Laird Red Sky in the Morning; Kiss the Dust
D H Lawrence The Fox and The Virgin and the Gypsy; Selected Tales
Harper Lee To Kill a Mockingbird
Julius Lester Basketball Game
Ursula Le Guin A Wizard of Earthsea
C Day Lewis The Otterbury Incident
David Line Run for Your Life; Screaming High
Joan Lingard Across the Barricades; Into Exile; The Clearance; The File on Fraulein Berg
Penelope Lively The Ghost of Thomas Kempe
Jack London The Call of the Wild; White Fang
Bernard Mac Laverty Cal; The Best of Bernard Mac Laverty
Margaret Mahy The Haunting; The Catalogue of The Universe
Jan Mark Do You Read Me? Eight Short Stories
James Vance Marshall Walkabout
Somerset Maugham The Kite and Other Stories
Michael Morpurgo Waiting for Anya; My Friend Walter; The War of Jenkins' Ear

How many have you read?

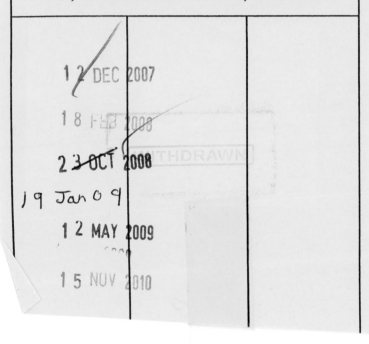